Jeffrey's Shorts

Geoffrey Crees

Numbers 6:24-26

instant apostle

First published in Great Britain in 2013

Instant Apostle
The Hub
3-5 Rickmansworth Road
Watford
Herts
WD18 0GX

Copyright © Geoffrey Crees 2013

All rights reserved. No portion of this book may be reproduced or transmitted in any form or by any means, electronic or mechanical, including photocopying, recording, or by any information storage and retrieval system, without permission in writing from the publisher.

British Library Cataloguing-in-Publication Data

A catalogue record for this book is available from the British Library

This book and all other Instant Apostle books are available from Instant Apostle:

Website: www.instantapostle.com
Email: info@instantapostle.com

ISBN 978-1-909728-12-7

Printed in Great Britain

Dedication

To Evie Iris with the prayer that as she grows, she will discover a living Christian faith for herself.

Contents

Introduction 8
Shorts for hairy legs 9
A French island 11
It must be summer! 16
And the winner is... 19
Graham, the greenhouse cleaner 30
CICPS 35
Lonely hearts 42
Aunt Daisy's legacy 49
One of our kettles is missing or The prodigal dog 58
So you were not 'done' as a child? 62
The red-top newspaper 83
Battle of the exes 98
Jeremy the journalist 113
The dying bishop 126
Getting the paperwork done 137
The invigilator 148
Visitors to the vicarage 158
The tumuli 166
The measure of a man 180
The damp BBQ 192

Acknowledgements

I am grateful to several friends who have provided useful comments especially Carol Baker, Rob Carruthers, Dorothy Crewdson and David Calliman.

Thank you too to Canon Gordon Oliver for suggestions, Manoj Raithatha, Nigel Freeman and Nicki Copeland of Instant Apostle for willingness to publish, and Gerald Paine for hospitality.

My thanks to Steve Jones, pastor at Forest Gate Church, Mitcheldean for the book cover, and above all to my dear wife Jean for deciphering my almost illegible script and typing and retyping many times! I owe each one a great debt of gratitude.

Also by Geoffrey Crees:
Where Was God Last Friday?
(Hodder & Stoughton, 1995, ISBN 0 340 63048 5)

Introduction

Few things compare with the pleasure of settling down to read a good book. It takes time and there is not always the space or possibility of doing so, and that is where the book of short stories comes into its own.

But why write a book, long or short? It is often said that there is 'a book in all of us'. I have certainly had fun writing these accounts and have even managed more than a smile to myself. Good humour is an essential part of life and certainly of the Christian life of faith, helping us see things in new light. Long may it continue.

I trust that in reading the stories in this book many of your doubts and disbeliefs will be gently challenged and your curiosity to search further ignited.

GEOFFREY CREES, Forest of Dean, autumn 2013

Disclaimer: All these situations and characters are fictitious. Some are based on personal experiences and some are amalgams of observations over many years.

Shorts for hairy legs

Carrie boarded the bus to Gloucester and duly zapped her bus pass on the machine in front of the driver, who was murmuring to himself that, even now, he could not get used to this new way of doing things.

Carrie found a seat next to Deidre whom she knew as a regular member of a local Anglican church. 'Any sign of a new vicar yet?' she asked.

'No,' replied Deidre. 'We had one round of interviews but nothing came of it. It's more than two years since Henry left – he was a nice man – don't see why he had to move.' Hardly pausing for breath, she continued, 'Anyway, I'm off to see the eye specialist at the hospital. I have to go every month; it's a degenerative condition called *rhesus pigmentosis*. I do a bit of shopping on the way back, so it makes quite a nice outing!'

Carrie thought a monthly trip to the hospital didn't sound like much of an outing, but she kept quiet about her own plans for the day. Deidre, however, was in no mood to close the conversation. 'How about you? Where are you going?' Without a pause, she immediately answered her own question. 'Into the town, I guess. I always say these drivers are so polite, not like those where my sister lives. She was only saying the other day that she wished their drivers could be like ours; we get much nicer types our way, and better looking too!'

Carrie was still wondering if she was going to get a word in when Deidre turned to her and asked, 'Don't suppose you have eye problems, do you?' It was more of a statement than a question, and then she continued, 'Is Seph still wearing his shorts? They suit him – especially with those hairy legs. Oh, I do like hairy legs!'

As the bus drew into the station and the passengers prepared to get off, Deidre got up saying, 'It's been nice seeing you again. I enjoyed our conversation.'

'What conversation?' Carrie asked herself. Deidre had posed three questions, one of which she had answered herself, and there had been no chance to reply to the other two.

'Why are people so interested in themselves and so little in others?' Carrie pondered as she made her way to the cardiology department at the hospital, where she faced the prospect of major surgery. How Christian is it not to listen? What would Jesus have done?

Back home, Carrie made herself a cup of tea and thought about the day. The heart specialist had been kindness itself, but there were loads of unanswered questions going around in her mind, questions she wanted to share with someone: Can I face life-threatening surgery? What will the family think? How will I tell my aged widowed mother who thinks most, if not all, doctors are crooks. In all her 85 years she has hardly ever had to trouble the medical profession.

She surveyed her husband's photograph and wished for the umpteenth time since the photo had been taken three years ago that he were still alive. He looked handsome in shorts – real ones – not those long Bermuda things, but ones that really showed up his muscular and, yes, hairy legs. She longed to be able to hug him, and them. Quite stupid. In fact, downright stupid.

Just then the door opened and in bounced her beloved bearded collie. 'Hello Seph, come to your mum, my precious!' she said.

'It's time you stopped treating that animal as a human being,' intoned the formidable voice of her mother. 'And why, oh why, do you insist on dressing him in those ridiculous shorts?'

A French island

Gordon had inherited a very large sum of money from his parents who had won it on the National Lottery many years before. Since they died he had continued to live in the modest three-bedroomed bungalow, on his own except for his elderly cat called Prescott. At the age of 66 and newly retired, he wondered what the future offered – if, indeed, there was a future.

He had a number of friends at the Baptist church he went to most Sundays and he enjoyed the worship, teaching and fellowship, but life was pretty empty. Oh yes, he had plenty of hobbies to fill his time and a number of people he counted as friends, especially in the home group he went to once a fortnight. But they were all younger than him and he sometimes felt they patronised him, especially when they invited him out at Christmas. 'We can't leave Gordon on his own at Christmas,' was the cry of the pastor which echoed in the ears of many church members. However, New Year's Eve was a different story, and he spent it alone. Friends from the office used to pop in during the first few months of his retirement, but the visits became fewer as time went by.

What should he do with his life and, especially, the money he had acquired? He had felt it his Christian duty to dispose of it responsibly, but that still left a sizeable figure in the bank and building society. It was so sad that his parents had had hardly any time to enjoy it before they died. What is more, who could share his wealth? He imagined himself as a character in a book or film called *The Lonely Millionaire*. Perhaps he should give it all away and just live on his company and state pensions.

In the past Gordon had enjoyed good relationships with

members of the opposite sex. In fact, he was once nearly engaged, but that had ground to a halt when his company had posted him overseas.

What should he do? He wasn't really close enough to anyone to seek advice. The pastor at the church should be an obvious choice, but since all his gifts to the church and elsewhere had been anonymous he felt somewhat diffident in approaching the Rev Charles Palter, an erudite preacher with a real love of his Lord, but somehow lacking in real pastoral skills.

Perhaps he could invest in something which could be of stimulating interest. And then he found something on the internet: 'Islands for sale'.

Being a real landlubber Gordon had only a passing interest in the sea. He scrolled through the list: Arkisig off the coast of Norway, Bacmire in the Hebrides, Torvie off the coast of Ireland, and so the list went on, all with clear descriptions and mostly unsuitable, but all at prices he could easily afford. Just imagine it – me, Gordon Westwell, owner of an island! he thought.

Then, the name Le Treviot came up. Uninhabited but with one small cottage occasionally visited in the summer. Six hectares, mostly heather, with one small sandy beach, 15 kilometres from Cannes in the Med.

Things moved rapidly after that and, despite the complexities of the French legal system, within two months he was the proud owner of Le Treviot!

Time to take a trip to Cannes, thought Gordon soon after. So with flights booked, car hired and hotel paid for, he was heading for the neighbouring island of Ile St Honorat via a boat service from Cannes.

After dinner at his small but comfortable hotel Gordon enquired about getting to Le Treviot. The hotel owner, François, who fortunately spoke reasonable English compared to Gordon's poor schoolboy French, told him Gustof at the harbour would most likely be willing to take him in the morning. 'It's only eight kilometres but it can be a bit choppy at times. Why do you want to go there? Nobody has lived there for at least ten years – it's been up for sale nearly all that time. Many people round here say it's haunted.'

Gordon coughed and spluttered, 'Well, I'm the new owner.'

'My God!' exclaimed the hotel proprietor. 'Fancy an Englishman buying the island even before he has seen it. Congratulations! Come have a Pastis on the house and I will tell you all I know about Le Treviot. Have you got a wife in England who will join you?'

Gordon replied with some sadness that there was no one with whom he could share his new manor. François thought about the single women in the village who might jump at the opportunity, but he was sure that the reputation of Le Treviot would put them off.

The day dawned sunny and bright and the road to the harbour was lined with blossom-filled trees. The sea sparkled in the sunlight and Gordon found Gustof waiting for him with his outboard chugging, ready for the trip. Gordon had come well prepared, having stocked up at the local supermarché with plenty of food, a stove, camping gas, lamps and, not least, a week's supply of toilet rolls. Gustof spoke very little English but was able to enquire, 'How long for?' as he clasped Gordon's generous 50-euro note.

'Two days,' replied Gordon. 'Pick me up this time on Thursday.'

Gordon was ecstatic to discover how green the island was in early spring. The cottage, though long abandoned, had most of its windows intact, though the door creaked and lacked a key for the lock.

A French notice said, 'Bienvenue. Spring water up the hill to the right. Toilet is round the back – empty each week,' and there were a number of other notices Gordon found hard to decipher. He thought to himself, I don't think I ever dreamed of living on a desert island, let alone owning one!

Apart from Mrs Thomas next door who had promised to feed the cat for a couple of days, no one at all even knew he was away, let alone about his adventure or that he was now the proud owner of a French island. Good luck, good fortune or God's blessing? He just did not know – all he did know was that he felt more at peace than he had for a long time. Back home in Sanderford was all very nice, but here he was enjoying the warm early spring sunshine, swimming in clear blue water and exploring his new acquisition. The fact that the place lacked any proper furniture did little to dampen his enthusiasm as he slept dreamlessly each night under the two blankets he had managed to cram into his travel bags.

The time seemed to fly by and all too soon he heard the chug of the outboard motor when Gustof arrived to transport him back to the hotel.

What strange thoughts were going through Gordon's mind as he prepared to board the aircraft at Cannes airport. The dominant one was that he had been all alone for 48 hours on a strange island with no one within eight kilometres, and yet he had enjoyed a feeling of peace which had been escaping him for many years. Much as he often longed for human company, on the island he had felt a companionship which was not human but very real. Could he have been found by God, in whom he had wanted to believe for years but to whom he could never really commit himself? He could not wait to return to the island, but should he come alone again or try to find a companion to share this perfect place with him? How to decide...

Such were his thoughts on the flight home. Eventually Robinson Crusoe had found a Man Friday – perhaps there was a Girl Friday available. Maybe he could take Mrs Thomas, but no, that would be stretching it too far! God – yes, God would be with him in his somewhat lonely world, but he wished for – oh, he desperately wanted – a companionable human being.

The air steward noticed he had tears in his eyes as the plane landed, and wondered why, but she kept her thoughts to herself.

To be continued…

It must be summer!

'It must be summer!' cried Petra as Jeffrey appeared at her house. Jeffrey was wearing his shorts. A murmur rang round the female coffee drinkers in Petra's front room – approval, amazement, or simply surprise as the group reassembled for the first time after the Easter break. Only Zoe did not join in with the comments on the brown hairy legs that had arrived and were now sitting opposite her. Although she said nothing, the other members of the group sensed her disquiet.

Jeffrey felt the vibes so he went to the kitchen to top up his coffee, and on return he found a seat out of Zoe's line of vision. 'Good evening, everyone,' said Petra cheerfully. 'Did you have a good Easter?' Without waiting for a reply she continued that she and Bruce had enjoyed a fabulous time skiing in the Dolomites, but then continued with a long report as to how the baggage handlers had gone on strike, how Bruce had booked a cheaper hotel and how cold the room had been, how grumpy the staff were, how Bruce had lost his passport only to find it much later in the lining of his suitcase. 'I told him,' cried Petra, 'I'll have to come home without you.'

Although they had been married some 20 years, Petra's little hobby seemed to be running her husband down. The others in the group took it in their stride but no one said openly what they all felt: that the denigration of one's spouse was, at the least, unkind and not in line with the Christian ethos of the group.

Week after week Petra's barbed comments and complaints fell on stony ground until, at last, Robin, who generally contributed little to the discussion, felt he could take it no longer. He managed to overcome his shyness to say in as authoritative a tone as he could muster, and in as caring a way as he could find, 'Petra, dear, Bruce isn't here to defend himself. I do think you are being hard on him.'

'You're not married to him,' spat back Petra. 'You try living with him – then you'd find out what he's really like.'

All thoughts of Jeffrey's shorts disappeared as the group tried to wrestle with the outburst. An embarrassed hush fell on them all, broken by the doorbell as Clive and Jane arrived, late as usual.

'What have we stepped into?' enquired Clive gently. That was just too much for Petra, who fled from the room in a flood of tears and locked herself in the downstairs loo. Nobody seemed sure what to do next.

'Let her be,' said George. 'She'll come round eventually.'

'Shall we get on with tonight's study?' Simon, the designated leader of the group, suggested meekly. 'You remember our pastor spoke on conflict resolution last Sunday. I didn't understand it but I have the CD if anybody cares to listen to it.'

Angela, George's wife, proposed, 'I've got my guitar here. Let's sing "Praise Him, praise Him in every circumstance, praise Him in melody and dance". Come on, we all know it.'

'Shut up!' shouted Robin. 'Why are we trying to carry on as usual when Petra is crying her heart out in the loo?'

'Shall we pray?' responded Simon.

'What do you suggest?' cried several voices in unison. '"Lord, get Petra out of the loo"?'

Simon, who didn't really enjoy the role of leader but had agreed to take it on when no one else wanted it, offered to walk along the passageway of the rather large Victorian house to try and talk to Petra.

'Petra, are you in there?' he enquired.

Silence.

He tried again. 'Petra, are you there?' he pleaded.

'Of course I bloody well am. Where else do you think I'd be?'

Simon, taken aback by all this, could not really say anything, shocked as he was by Petra's latest outburst. Zoe appeared at Simon's elbow. 'Petra, dear, would you like a cup of tea?'

'Go away,' came the sharp retort from within.

Jeffrey joined the pair outside the loo door. 'Petra, could you... George – you know he has a waterworks problem and he needs to go urgently.' George usually kept quiet about his 'waterworks' problem and often left early in order not to embarrass the others.

'Tell him to go upstairs,' came the reply from within.

'Well, you know George has a dodgy leg and finds climbing stairs very difficult And anyway, didn't you say that the upstairs cistern is kaput?'

How can I break this impasse? thought Simon, wearing the leadership mantle. It's a stalemate. Just then they heard a key in the door. As it opened, they saw Bruce standing there, smiling broadly.

'Hello, everybody. I've come to join you. I hear from Petra what a happy, loving group you are and I want to be part of such a crowd. I've brought my Bible.'

At that point the loo door flew open and Petra, still full of tears, fell with loud sobs into his welcoming arms.

'Had a good study, Dad?' asked Liz as George got home.

'Very interesting,' said George with a whimsical smile.

'What were you studying?'

'Conflict resolution,' he replied.

And the winner is...

The Awards Committee of the BAABS Society (British Animals and Birds Society) met in London to discuss and vote on the winner of this year's 'Naturalist of the Year'. The cup, originally donated by Lord Allingburgh, the famous environmentalist, was now sponsored by Air Venturscope.

Each region had nominated their preferred candidate. For the South-west it was Helen Simpson, 22, for her work with injured swans. The name suggested by the South-east was Stephen How-Jones, 23, who had made a special study of moles and their habits. The choice of the Midland region was Margaret Davison, 64, who had made owl nesting her chosen subject; and Peter James, 17, in the North-west had gleaned a lot of information about the habits of eels. The North-east elected Mark Turney, 28, with his recorded observations of gannets on Flamborough Head. Graham Mackie, 18, was the selection of southern Scotland with records of urban foxes. The north of Scotland chose Susan McDowell, 24, from the Isle of Lewis for her study of kittiwakes. Northern Ireland was to be represented by Ian Dulany, 38, who spent as much of the year as his job allowed studying grey seals. Finally, for Wales, Kathy Thomas, 16, had gathered a huge amount of statistics on peregrine falcons.

So these nine names appeared on the agenda of the committee. The chairman, having called the group to order, said, 'You have nine candidates for this prestigious award.' Sir Marcus Rigby had chaired this decision-making body, which consisted of members representing the various regions, for more years than he could remember.

The members perused their agenda papers. No one spoke

for a while so Sir Marcus continued. 'You have all seen the submissions. Jolly good work I say by all of them.' All this said in his best military voice.

Eventually the member for Wales found his voice and championed the name of the youngest candidate, Kathy Thomas. At this, each member began speaking in favour of their own local candidate. This was too much for Sir Marcus, who rapped the table with his knuckles which, in fact, hurt quite a bit, but with his Guards background he did not dare to show it.

'Quiet please!' he bellowed. 'You have your voting papers before you. You must have read the claims of each candidate and know them backwards by now. I am afraid it is the quite stupid system of PR.' Sir Marcus was every inch a traditionalist. 'If first past the post was good enough for Churchill, it's good enough for me,' he was heard to mutter. So after a good deal of chattering and widespread conversation, each member duly marked their voting paper.

'Remind me, my dear,' Sir Marcus whispered audibly to Beatrice, who had been ordered to take the minutes by the chief secretary of the society, 'what do we do next?' He was anxious to get everything over and done with as he had a lunch appointment at his club.

Beatrice was used to the chairman losing his place, and sometimes his rag as well. Quietly, and with an efficiency that belied her years, she told him, 'The top three are then voted for again. I have the extra voting papers here.'

'Harrumph,' Sir Marcus coughed impatiently. Beatrice collected the voting papers and handed them to the chairman. As was expected, each region had voted for their own candidate, but Kathy Thomas had four extra votes, Margaret Davison had an extra three and Ian Dulany two extra.

Beatrice soon had a new voting slip in the hand of each member and the procedure began again, but this time with considerable conversation around the table, which the more uncouth among them might describe as 'horse trading'. Others looked again through the 300–400 word essays each candidate had supplied.

Votes were soon collected and Beatrice whispered in Sir Marcus' ear (something he found quite pleasant), 'It's Margaret Davison.'

The meeting fell silent as Sir Marcus announced the name of the winner. He liked this part as he could exert his authority. 'The candidate you have chosen is Margaret Davison, whose mini treatise on the nesting habits of owls makes her a worthy winner. You will no doubt have read her personal profile. Beatrice will, of course, notify her, and the presentation of the Allingburgh Cup will be made at the annual dinner at the Forchester Hotel on the 26th of next month. What is it Beatrice?' Sir Marcus was aware that his lunch appointment was almost upon him, and besides that, he was getting hungry.

'No. It's the 27th at 7pm precisely.'

Having had his ear bent by the ever-efficient Beatrice, Sir Marcus corrected himself. 'Must dash – good show.' He collected his papers and headed for the door where his chauffeur was dutifully waiting.

The BAABS envelope was pushed through Margaret's letterbox and landed on the floor. Kettle – her Lhasa Apso pup – sniffed and decided to ignore it. Margaret retrieved it and discovered, to her great surprise, that she was the winner of 'Naturalist of the Year' and that she had been sent complimentary tickets for the Gala Dinner for herself and a friend in London on the 27th. She was thrilled and delighted as nothing like this had ever happened to her before, in all her 64 years. She had now been retired quite a while and busied herself with her field studies and life in her local church where she did not lack friends, although none came as close as Dick, who had been killed in the Falklands War.

After Dick's death Margaret had spent time questioning the purposes of God, but had now resigned herself to the single life. True, she had friends from her days at BT, as well as Dave who had recently started coming to the church and who on the previous Sunday had asked her out.

At my age? she thought as she politely refused, but secretly hoping that he just might ask her again. She studied herself in the full length mirror. 'Not bad,' she said to herself, 'still slim, very little grey hair. I could pass for 50 and a bit,' before taking Kettle for his morning stroll.

After the stroll she typed out her acceptance but had to pause when she noticed her guest had to be named. She picked up the phone. 'Kate, are you there?' Her best friend, with whom she had shared countless holidays, answered. Margaret was all 'bubble and squeak' as she told Kate the good news.

'That's wonderful! Congratulations, Marge.' Kate was the only one in their circle of friends to call her Marge.

'Kate will you come with me to the gala dinner and presentation on the 27th?'

There was a long pause while Kate looked through her diary. 'Sorry, Marge. I'm looking after Jane's kids that week. She and George are off to Barbados.'

'Well, never mind,' replied a disappointed Margaret. 'I expect someone else will come. I'll ask around at church on Sunday. Goodbye and God bless.'

Suddenly the thought struck her: why not ask Dave? No, it's ridiculous and I hardly know him. I don't want him getting the wrong idea. Men are always thinking two steps ahead; even some so-called Christian men can't think in terms of just simple friendship.

So she just juggled the thought around in her brain until she was too worried even to pray about it. It was the 18th already, and replies had to be in by the first of next month. She pondered over it all evening, even considering declining the invitation, although the thought that a car would be provided all the way to London, plus overnight accommodation in a four-star hotel, was very appealing.

She continued in this mode for over a week, doing all her normal things, walking Kettle and going to her home group on Thursday evening. At the end of the evening, as they all sat drinking tea or coffee, she said quietly, 'I have something to share with the group.' Margaret was not a shy person and could never be accused of hiding her light under a bushel, and soon they all knew of her success.

Congratulations were soon flowing from everyone there. Margaret continued, 'The only trouble is, I don't know who to take. Kate's looking after her daughter's children that week and I don't know who else to ask.' It so happened that she was the only single in the group that week. Janice, a widow, came along sometimes, but it was usually just the five couples and Margaret.

The prayer time took a slightly different slant from usual. The general gist was along the lines that if the Lord wanted Margaret to go, then He should please provide a friend to go with her.

Back home, Margaret phoned Janice to enquire as to her well-being. 'I'm OK,' was the reply, 'but it's just that at the group I don't seem to belong and I don't get much out of it. I don't want to be critical but you seem to be family and I feel excluded by the others sometimes.'

'Don't say that,' Margaret quickly replied. 'You are as much loved as anyone in the group. I was wondering, I wonder…' Her voice trailed off. Somehow she felt that Janice was not the right person to accompany her to London.

'Hello there, are you hoping to move?' Margaret was looking at the details in an estate agent's window, which she often did after her weekly shopping trip. She turned round to see Dave smiling at her.

'Er, no – not really,' she stammered. 'I just like to window gaze, that's all.'

'Would you like a coffee? It's a while before I catch my train,' asked Dave.

'No, but thanks all the same,' said Margaret, although she really wanted to say yes. 'I have to get home to take Kettle out. See you on Sunday,' was all she could manage, noticing how disappointed Dave seemed. 'Perhaps another time,' she added encouragingly. Of course, it wasn't quite true, as Kettle had enjoyed a good walk before Margaret had gone into town, but it seemed a convenient excuse.

Two days later, with the deadline for the acceptance due, she picked up the phone and tried Dave's number. 'The person you are calling is on the phone. Please try later,' the disembodied voice intoned. Margaret had taken the precaution of dialling 141 before ringing his number, so that Dave would, she hoped, not know she had rung if she lost her nerve and put the phone down before he picked up. Once more she picked up the phone, only to put it down again. She now resolved that the only thing she could do was to send a reply that she was unable to attend, which plainly was not true. She assumed the trophy would then be sent to her or would be presented by the chairman of her local BAABS group.

The loud ring of her phone broke into her musings. Oh no, she thought, perhaps Dave had somehow found that she had called and was calling back. Should she answer it? Should she ignore it? Unfortunately she did not have a machine modern enough to show who was ringing. Whoever they were, they were very persistent.

Eventually, after the ringing ceased, she switched on the answerphone and almost immediately the ringing began again.

The answerphone clicked in and she listened to the voice at the other end. 'This is Mike Harrod from the *Tamworth Times*. We hear you have won Naturalist of the Year and we would like to come and interview you and take a few pictures for next week's edition.'

For the first time in many years, Margaret regretted her single status. She dialled Kate who answered immediately. 'Kate, help!' she cried. 'The local press want to interview me and I'm scared they'll ask all sorts of embarrassing questions. I really think I ought to opt out of this whole business and let someone else get the award. After all, I only spent a few nights watching the owls' nest in Oxhope Woods – a few very late ones and a few very early mornings.'

'Let them come,' was Kate's firm reply, and so they did.

Mike Harrod and his photographer, Mark Hooper, were enquiring, pleasant and well behaved – not at all how Margaret expected the media to act. Photos taken, interview taped – Mike Harrod doubled up for the local radio station – and off they went, but not before Mike had dropped the bombshell: 'Of course,' he said, 'we shall be sending someone to the Forchester Hotel to cover the presentation. Do you know who you will be taking as your guest?'

Margaret shut the door and sat down, and tears came to her eyes. Why did I ever enter this competition? What was I thinking? It was getting very complicated. Why, oh why, have I got myself into this mess? She tried Kate again, but there was only the answer phone. I only have a week to reply, she panicked.

At church on Sunday, those who had heard about the award – and there were many – surrounded Margaret to congratulate her. As is the way of things, someone asked pertinently who she was taking as her guest.

'I don't know,' was Margaret's mumbled reply. 'I don't know if I'm even going at all.'

'But you must,' cried half a dozen voices in unison, including Dave's.

'It's good news for our town and maybe a little "street cred" for our church,' said the vicar. He was always looking for street cred for St Agatha's.

The evening before the deadline, Margaret's quandary deepened. She hovered over the phone, started to dial Dave's number and then put the phone down, only to pick it up again half an hour later. Eventually courage kicked in and she got through to Dave. She hesitated and began diffidently, 'Dave, you know I have won this award, and I... I can take someone with me to the presentation, and I was wondering if you would be able to go with me? It's an awful cheek, I know.'

For the first time in many years Margaret felt herself blushing. 'Of course I'll come. I somehow hoped you might ask me,' was Dave's instant reply. They chatted for a while and arranged to meet the next day. The day the reply had to be posted.

Coffee in the Corner Café never tasted so good. Margaret insisted on paying for herself and Dave. Her next thought was, Help, I'll need a new dress. I can't ask Dave to help me choose. What does he know about women? She realised that she knew very little about him. He was tall, had a slight military bearing and had all the attributes of a gentleman. But what was his background? Had he ever been married? Perhaps he was still married! What the heck, she thought. 'Come with me next week so we can approve my new dress.'

'Only if I pay for lunch,' was Dave's reply.

Cheltenham had many dress shops and Margaret tried on dozens. Dave, ever patient, refused the 'bored husband's chair' in one shop. He was the epitome of politeness, even if he wasn't her husband.

At Spendless Dresses a red dress fitted perfectly. Even the

over-fussy assistant was impressed. 'I can't wear this!' cried Margaret, 'I'm too old for a strapless dress.'

'Oh no you're not,' chorused the duet of Dave and the assistant. 'You look lovely.'

'But I've never worn anything so provocative, and at 64 I'm not going to start now!' But Dave and the assistant persisted, and so the purchase was made.

Over lunch Dave revealed a little of his personal history – his naval career, cut short by an accident to his spine; his marriage to Joanne cut short by her premature death; his loneliness conquered more than a little by the love of God. Suddenly Margaret thought, I'll be in the papers again. They can't photograph me in that dress; all the people in the street will see it, not least the vicar and the people at St Agatha's.

'Dave,' she said as firmly as she could. 'I have to go back and change that dress – it's not becoming of a woman my age!'

'Oh no you don't. And besides, I'm paying for it. I arranged it with that fussy old assistant when your back was turned.'

Margaret was shocked. 'Fussy old assistant? She looked half my age!'

Early on the afternoon of the special day, Kate dropped in to give her approval to the outfit. 'Stunning!' was her verdict.

The chauffeur-driven car duly arrived. It was Sir Marcus' own car and chauffeur. Dave was dressed in his tuxedo and looked very handsome. So the pair were whisked off to London to a prime seat at the dinner just below the top table. Speeches duly followed, including a long boring one by Sir Marcus. A less boring one was made by the BAABS secretary, Elaine Blunt, and a highly amusing one by Sir David Allingburgh who duly informed the assembled company that it had been a very close competition and announced the winner as Margaret Davison from the Midland region who lives in Tamworth.

So Margaret was escorted, very gingerly and shyly, to the

rostrum to receive her prize. With some effort she held the gold-plated cup aloft while she held the miniature (for her to keep) in her left hand. The assembled company clapped and cameras flashed. A TV camera from the Midlands area zoomed in and she smiled shyly.

It seemed hours later when they finally got to her room in the hotel and she put the trophy on the dressing table. There in large letters was engraved on the cup, 'Awarded to Margaret Davison: *Naturist* of the Year'.

She and Dave could not believe their eyes. The engraver had made a dreadful mistake! They said a tired goodnight and Dave went to his own room. Margaret eventually dropped off to a troubled sleep, wondering how on earth she was going to face the world, let alone her friends at the Ornithological Society and the church! What would the neighbours think?

Early the next morning a newspaper was pushed under her door. She picked it up and was aghast to find that she was front page news! It was still early but the phone rang; it was Mike from the *Tamworth Times*.

'Can I have a few comments please?' he asked. Mike already knew about the engraving error – he had seen the headlines in the nationals saying 'Engraving error'. 'Who the L left it out?' was one of the red top headlines, not to mention, 'When did Margaret bare all for the birds?' 'Owl watching in the buff'. And so they went on. Dave knocked on the door and they went down to breakfast, but not before an army of photographers were flashing their cameras, anxious not to miss their five minutes of fun and Margaret's chagrin.

Most of the journey back to Tamworth was spent in silence. Eventually Dave held Margaret's hand and she grasped it tightly. Arriving back they thanked the chauffeur and disappeared into Margaret's bungalow. There was a message from Kate full of congratulations and sympathy, together with the remark that the engraver should get the sack, but that the mistake could soon be put right. Before they had time to even sit down, the phone rang; it was Sir Marcus' secretary. 'Just one moment please,' she said and then Sir Marcus was speaking, full of apologies.

'Should have checked the damn thing myself,' he said. 'Come up to my club before too long and we can have dinner together,' was his somewhat half-hearted invitation.

The next phone call was a voice in a rather different tone. 'Hi, I'm Jamie of the *Front Page*. You must have heard of us – we do glossy pics, not quite top-shelf stuff. Look, we can make you an offer you can't refuse. You looked stunning in that red dress last night and we'd like to photograph what's underneath. It'll be a four-figure sum!'

Margaret slammed the phone down – something she had never done before. Her composure completely disappeared. She whirled round and fell into the arms of the ever-patient Dave.

'Naturist or Naturalist of the Year, I don't care,' he said. 'I just want you to marry me.'

'Only if you get down on one knee,' was Margaret's rather limp reply.

Graham, the greenhouse cleaner

If you are a gardener I'm sure you'll agree there are some horticultural tasks that are pleasant to do and some that are real chores – like cleaning the greenhouse. The tomatoes, cucumbers, melons and aubergines are all harvested, and what is left is a sad and sorry mess. Yes, the chrysanths have to be brought in, together with anything the frost will damage, such as the pelargoniums. Graham looked at the tangle of decaying material and decided it was best left to another day.

'You are a putter-offer,' said Joan. Graham queried this, but in his heart of hearts he knew it to be true. 'If you don't do it, I'll get someone to do it for us,' was his wife's terse comment. In a sombre tone she added, 'I hope you'll do the downstairs windows as well while you're at it.'

Now cleaning windows was not really Graham's forte. In spite of George Formby's song ringing in his memory, he would rather pick up Lucky's poo than clean windows. His wife's final riposte before she let the subject drop was, 'Remember last year when you fell through and ended up in hospital.'

'Got the scars to prove it,' muttered Graham.

'Doesn't look too bad if I look at the other side of your face,' was her final and unsympathetic word on the matter.

The next day dawned bright and fine and so Graham headed for his beloved greenhouse – not to sow and plant or harvest, but to clean.

Soon a pile of trays, old growbags and rolls of bubble wrap were piled outside the door, not to mention seed packets and pots of various sizes which had all accumulated during the summer. Graham's heart and spirit sank lower as the pile grew larger. I never had a greenhouse before I retired, he thought to himself, and now I wonder if it's worth it after all. Tomatoes and cucumbers are easy to buy in the supermarket; as for aubergines – they're hit and miss; same goes for melons.

Yes, in his youth, he had heard countless sermons on getting rid of the rubbish in our lives, but this was different. 'Ah! That slug needs disposing of,' he grunted as he used his wellington boot. Despite all his efforts with slug pellets and insect repellent during the summer they had still invaded the greenhouse. No wonder Joan didn't exactly volunteer to help. The next pest to be dealt with was a leather jacket.

'How are you getting on, dear?' asked a pleasant voice over a steaming cup of coffee. Before Graham could answer, she continued, 'Think of all the wonderful crops we've had, and will have next year. All those slugs and other intruders won't stand a chance once it's clean and tidy.'

'Didn't do a great deal of good this year,' was Graham's rather grumpy reply. 'Don't know why I bother really.'

Not to be silenced, Joan continued, 'You bother because it's *your* greenhouse and you know it gets you out from under my feet, same as when you disappear into the garage for hours. Anyway, I'm off to the home group. At least I'll get some intelligent conversation there.'

Graham was about to reply but she had already disappeared. Left alone, he set to work, scrubbing the concrete floor with disinfectant and applying Joan's window cleaner to the sometimes green slimy windows. He was not enjoying himself and was interrupted by his neighbour, Cedric, leaning over the fence. 'You look busy,' was his unhelpful comment. Now if there was one thing that was guaranteed to annoy Graham, it was being labelled 'busy'.

'No, not really,' was his reply, in a tone showing that his grumpiness had not entirely evaporated.

'Come on, Graham, let's get some ale inside us.'

The temptation to nip off for a 'quick half' was too great, and they were soon in a corner of the local Carpenters Arms. Graham stared into the pint Cedric had planted before him.

'Get this down your gullet. It'll clear your head before Joan comes home.'

'I said a swift half, Ced. Not a pint. Nevertheless, here's to married life – what there is of it! Do you know, Ced, we've been married these past 40 years, seen the kids grow up and yet, just recently, she seems a stranger to me. She goes off to her church meetings on Sundays. I have to get the lunch these days! Wednesdays it's ladies' fellowship, Thursday is home group and now she's on a couple of committees. Don't know what she sees in all this. It's not that I don't believe, but it's really for the kids and old people. It's causing a real rift, this religion stuff. I could go and on.'

'You are,' interrupted Cedric. 'Have another pint and you'll feel better.'

Graham continued gloomily, 'It's not that there's another man in her life – mind you, about six months ago she did come home and say just that! I said – and for once I swore – I said I'd ring that b---- pastor's neck. How dare he interfere in our lives – he's half our age. When I did calm down, she said, "No, it's not Pastor Brown – though he is rather handsome – no, it's Jesus in my life!" You could have knocked me down with a spade. Don't get it. Do you, Ced?'

'No mate, though my nephew thinks much the same. He plays drums in some religious band. I thought drum kits were for the Sally Army. Now that's what I call real religion – even if they dress up in those funny uniforms. My nephew used to be into drugs and was always out of work; now he's a changed lad.'

'Joan's never been into drugs,' reflected Graham, 'at least as far as I know.' Then realising the time, the two decided they had better get back before their respective wives discovered their absence.

'Have a good afternoon, dear?' Graham asked.

Joan was staggered. It was the first time ever that Graham had enquired about her church activities. 'Yes, it was very interesting. How have you been getting on?

'OK,' came the reply, as Graham realised he had not got very far in cleaning the greenhouse, but since it was out of sight from the bungalow Joan could not see how little progress had been made.

'What was it all about?' A couple of pints of ale had loosened Graham's tongue just a little. Joan thought it rather odd but suspected nothing as to where Graham had spent the afternoon. She didn't know where to start.

'It was about...' she trailed off. 'I need to go to the loo.'

Once out of sight she got out her mobile. 'Patsie, help!' she cried down the phone. 'Graham's asking what the meeting was about. He's never done that before – what do I say?'

'Just answer his questions and I'll go and pray about it,' Patsie's calm voice replied.

'You were a long time in the loo. Are you alright?' was Graham's unsuspecting comment.

'It's Freda's rock cakes – they bung me up a bit.'

Graham persisted. 'You were going to let me know what the meeting was all about. Come on, spill the beans. It wasn't just about recipes for rock cakes, was it?'

At this Joan half smiled and then suddenly burst into tears. This was too much for Graham, who threw his arms around her and they sunk back onto the sofa. 'Tell me, darling, what you have to say.' Joan was amazed. Graham had not called her darling in decades, and in recent years he had hardly put his arms around her.

'It was... it was... well, it was...' mumbled Joan through her tears.

'Go on,' encouraged Graham.

'It was about praying for our unbelieving husbands.' The words came out in a rush.

'I've never said I don't believe; I just don't get this Jesus in your life stuff! So did you pray for me, then?'

'Yes we did,' replied Joan, feeling more confident.

'What do you mean, "*we* did"? And did God answer your prayers, then? Now you're not quite so sure,' said Graham trying not to be cynical.

Later that evening as they got undressed for bed, they discovered something different about each other, and for the first time for many a year they made love in a passionate and intoxicating way, almost as if they were newly married.

'Joan,' Graham said dreamily before they settled down to sleep. 'I think I might come with you on Sunday.'

'Graham, have you been drinking?' smiled Joan.

CICPS

'Jeffrey,' called the vicar, 'we need someone to go and represent us at the CICPS meeting – will you go? They've set up their national headquarters in Rock Street and have invited a representative from the local churches to go along to their meetings.'

'You know how I hate committee meetings, Shane,' replied Jeffrey. 'I'm afraid I volunteered you,' came the reply.

Shane was a very devout minister, but he had the prevailing weakness of almost always saying yes to any request and volunteering other people for tasks he could not, or more likely, did not want to undertake himself. In this case it was definitely the latter.

'They meet on Wednesday week. I'll give you their email address and you can reply and download the agenda. Jeffrey's heart sank. He did not want to go to another meeting, nor did he really understand what CICPS believed, even if they prefixed the title of their work by adding 'Christian'.

Jeffrey had always been sure that Christians should not live in holy huddles; they should get involved in the world. How else could they represent Christ among their fellow men and women? But he thought that going to a CICPS meeting was going a step too far.

'Jill,' he said to his wife, after their meal was ended, 'Shane has volunteered me to go to the next CICPS meeting. As you know they've set up in Rock Street.'

'I know, dear, I mentioned to Shane that you might be someone who could represent St Agatha's,' Jill replied.

'But it's just another meeting,' he protested.

'Well, go just this once – you're always going on about getting out into the world outside work or the golf club!'

Jeffrey thought it should be a matter for prayer, but words just would not come and, anyway, he knew better than to argue with either Shane or Jill – especially Jill.

Wednesday week came and all day long at the office Jeffrey had an awful sinking feeling in the pit of his stomach – is it right to go? His colleagues sensed he wasn't himself, but he dismissed any comments with, 'It must have been something I ate,' and so on. The response was to blame the staff canteen at lunchtime before they realised that Jeffrey rarely went there as he usually brought sandwiches into work.

He pushed the door of 38 Rock Street, a small ground-floor office in a block only ten minutes walk from home. 'Come in,' said a disembodied voice. 'You must be Jeffrey Armstrong. Rev Shane said you'd be coming to our meeting.' Jeffrey discovered that the voice belonged to Archie, whose bulky figure emerged from behind a filing cabinet. 'The others will be here in a moment. CICPS members are notorious latecomers.'

Black mark number one, thought Jeffrey, wishing he had never got involved in this exercise, but perhaps it would be better later on. At last the other six members arrived and arranged themselves around the table – all except Deidre, who eventually arrived breathless and harassed.

The group introduced themselves and said something of their background. Archie called the meeting to order, introduced Jeffrey, and called their attention to the agenda papers which all except Jeffrey seemed to have seen before – he had forgotten to download them.

'Any apologies? No, I can see we're all here. Minutes of the last meeting – can I take these as read?' Archie was brisk if not brusque. 'I take the silence to mean yes. I will duly sign them. And so to the main agenda. Item number one. I take it you have all read Rev Forrester Mackie's article in the *Tamworth Gazette*.' It was more a statement than a question.

Jeffrey knew Forrester slightly as he was pastor to an evangelical church on the new housing estate. His congregation appeared to be young, vigorous and growing in numbers. He had a reputation for clear and sometimes controversial statements.

The article was an abridged version of a sermon he had given some weeks ago and the editor had invited him to submit it for publication with the proviso that the paper could disclaim it and could print replies in the following week's letters page, along with a counterbalancing article of equal length. The paper's stance was all for balance.

The article's headline was, 'What does it mean to be truly gay?' It delved into the origins of the word, the percentage of people who would subscribe to be practising homosexuals, the legislation that had outlawed homophobia and so on. He then addressed the issue of biblical teaching in relation to Leviticus 18:22 and 1 Corinthians 6:9. He understood the need for love and forgiveness, said such practices were sinful and stressed the offer of a new life in Christ.

Jeffrey had indeed read the article, which his wife had thrust in front of him. He did not know what to think; he had little experience of meeting anyone who was not heterosexual like himself. He did recall someone at school in the sixth form saying he was 'coming out', but Jeffrey had never really understood it. His musings were brought to an abrupt end as the chairman tore verbally into the article and more volubly into Forrester Mackie. 'The man is an absolute bigot – don't know how the paper dares print such an article.'

There were murmurs of agreement round the table. Only one dissenting voice was heard. It was Freda. 'I think the *Gazette* said we could write in if we disagreed, and a counterbalancing article will appear next week,' she said.

'Too late; the damage has been done,' stormed the chairman. 'We've fought for years for our rights and now this little upstart has destroyed all we stand for.'

Freda – who had been emboldened by her first contribution to the proceedings – said, 'I don't think you can call him little – he is 6'2" and did get a rugby blue at Oxford.'

The chairman was not to be placated. 'What on earth are we going to do about it now we're setting up our national office in the town – are we going to be told to clear off? That we're not welcome here?'

After another ten minutes of verbal abuse, he spotted Jeffrey. 'I take it you do not agree with Mr Mackie?'

Jeffrey was about to reply that he hated committee meetings and was beginning to dislike this one even more. Why on earth had he consented to attend? He had agreed to being involved in outside groups in theory, but this was different. Being a Christian in the marketplace was all very well but it did have its drawbacks, and this was one of them. Happily for him, before he could gather his thoughts and reply, the chairman said, 'I have drafted a reply to the *Tamworth Gazette*. I will read it to you:

'At the meeting of the committee of CICPS on Monday 9th November, it was agreed that we strongly refute the views expressed by Rev Forrester Mackie in last week's edition of the *Tamworth Gazette*. We call upon the editor to repudiate them or resign immediately. Such a stand should have no place in the Christian church, or indeed in our town. Members of CICPS will no longer purchase your scurrilous newspaper.'

But before the members could respond, there was a knock on the door and Deidre, being nearest, went to see who it was. She opened it and was surprised to see a smartly dressed woman standing there. 'Is this the meeting of CICPS,' she asked. 'Could I come in?'

'Yes, certainly,' replied Deidre. 'Come and take a seat. We

were just discussing a recent article in the local newspaper.'

'Name?' said the chairman in an abrupt manner, annoyed that someone should interrupt the flow of the committee's discussion.

The new arrival was in her late thirties and was very attractive, with medium length blonde hair and a trim figure. 'I'm Alice Mackie, the wife of Forrester Mackie. I'm sorry I'm late but I had to put the children to bed before I came. You know what it's like with children.'

A monastic silence descended on the company and there was both awkwardness and embarrassment. Jeffrey – sitting on the other side of the room, away from the chairman's eye – managed to suppress a giggle, but only just.

'Harrumph,' the chairman coughed. For the first time in the evening his confidence was somewhat dented. 'We were just discussing your husband's article in the *Tamworth Gazette*.'

'Oh yes,' smiled Alice. 'In fact, although it appeared in my husband's name, I really wrote it!' If there had been an embarrassed silence before, there was now one that was painful in the extreme. Alice looked around the room and every face except for Jeffrey's tried to avoid her smile, which most people found infectious and charming.

Sensing their difficulties, Alice continued, 'You see, Forrester is dyslexic; he has great difficulty putting pen to paper, let alone the computer keyboard. He is better now than when we first met.'

'May I ask where that was?' Jeffrey had found his voice, sensing the group did not know what to say or where to direct their gaze in the face of what seemed to be the most innocuous of charm offensives.

'At drama school. We were both budding actors. No money but the world at our feet, both dreaming of a life on the stage or TV. As you know, Forrester has a wonderful speaking voice and I was game for any role that was offered to me. However, the glitz and the glamour dimmed. We both graduated, found agents and waited to be signed up by London producers, but it never happened. Oh yes, we did get some parts in regional theatres, which we loved, but it didn't last more than 18 months. We got married, found we had to rely on our parents for support and wondered what the future held. And then a strange thing happened.'

At this point the chairman intervened. 'Mrs Mackie,' he said in his most formal voice, 'this is all most interesting, I don't think!'

The other members of the committee demurred and the meeting seemed on the verge of chaos. Eventually the chairman managed to regain some sort of order. Directing his attention to Alice, he said, 'Mrs Mackie, we were just finalising a resolution regarding the article in the *Tamworth Gazette* which was printed last week in *your* husband's name.' There was such an emphasis on *your* that it bordered on rudeness. Alice just smiled at him, and for once he found himself stuttering. 'We were just saying…' He looked around the group for support – support that was evaporating by the second.

'Go on,' encouraged Deidre.

'I… I don't think I… we… can really continue. Perhaps we were overreacting.' Gone was the pomposity, and instead the chairman was doing a good impression of a breathless goldfish.

'Well, I've had enough,' said Christopher, not having uttered a word all evening. 'Come on, Peter, let's get a beer.' And with that they departed.

'I'm off, too,' said Deidre, motioning to Rachel, who also had been silent all evening. 'Home we go.'

Jeffrey and Alice stood up; there was the slightest wink in his eye. The chairman made moves to leave, gathering up his papers and putting them in his briefcase. 'Perhaps there was a faint truth in some of the article after all. Good night,' he said.

Jeffrey and Alice looked at each other. 'This was meant to be a meeting of CICPS, wasn't it?' asked Jeffrey. 'The Christian International Cooperative Partnership Scheme, right?'

'Oh no!' said Alice, 'They're meeting next-door. CICPS stands for Christians in Civil Partnerships.'

'Hence the anger,' said Jeffrey wistfully.

'Was there any?' enquired Alice rather naively.

'You bet there was – but your entry changed everything,' replied Jeffrey.

'Let's go home. I'll ring Forrester to put the kettle on,' said Alice.

'Had a good evening?' enquired Jill when Jeffrey got home.

'Yes, but the first thing is to ring Shane and let him know what he let me in for!'

A week later a 'To Let' sign appeared on the CICPS door. The organisation seemed to have been stillborn, and a month later the Christian International Cooperative Partnership Scheme expanded their offices.

Lonely hearts

Gordon pondered the situation for days, indeed weeks. Here he was, the owner of the small island Le Treviot. He had bought it, seen it, lived on it for a few days, and now what? Was it possible that someone might come and join him for a month or two? He thought of people at church and quailed at the idea of asking anyone he knew. Not the least problem was that he wanted it to be a secret. He could trust François, the hotel owner, and Gustof, who had ferried him there and back a couple of weeks ago. But who else? Friends from his working days were ruled out, as well as various cousins.

Much as he disliked the idea, he decided in the end that the only way was to use the 'Lonely Hearts' column in a national newspaper. He drafted numerous scripts and made sure he deleted each one from his computer. The text he decided on was:

> Bachelor, 60s, proud owner of small French island, seeks female companion for three months: July–September. All found. Must be N/S with GSOH. Basic conditions only. Anyone with sense of adventure, reply PO Box 846.

(He chose 846 as it had been part of his home telephone number as a child.)

Within a few days he was inundated with replies. Help, how do I sort this lot out? What questions should I ask them? Can I possibly ask someone to help me without giving the game away? He started to sift through the pile. Some were obviously gold diggers; some were too old; some too young; some were trying to escape matrimonial unhappiness, and so on; until he wondered what he had let himself in for. But he went on, eliminating those who could not swim or disliked hot weather. But that still left about 41 possibilities. So he emailed each one requesting further details. Why were they free at that time? Would they send a photograph, etc? About 31 replied and he trawled through them, searching for the truth about each 'candidate'.

To finalise his choice he sent the remaining women a detailed questionnaire, and this time only eight replied. The choice was becoming much clearer after that: Evelyn, who had been a PE teacher and still played hockey for her local club – she was 61. There was Joy, 45, who had experience of mountaineering and deep-sea diving. She was currently unemployed. And finally Ann, also 45, the only one to say she was a Christian, who was getting over a broken engagement.

Gordon emailed each one to the effect that, subject to an interview at a hotel near their home, he would invite each one to spend a trial week on the island in June, all expenses paid. By now, of course, Gordon was himself having to answer many questions being asked of him. Evelyn wanted to know about sleeping arrangements and toilet facilities. Joy wanted to know if there was a boat and what the catering facilities were. Ann wanted to know something of Gordon's past and his spiritual state.

Each lady agreed to submit a confidential CV to him. When they arrived he was fascinated by each one, but dared not confide in anyone else about what he was planning to do; even less to consult another person as to who was the best candidate. This was so contrary to his nature, and indeed to his whole working life where he had always discussed things with others and worked in a team.

He put three folded pieces of paper with the names of Evelyn, Joy and Ann in a hat and popped round to Mrs Thomas next door. She thought it rather odd but, as asked, she pulled the pieces of paper out one by one. First out was Joy, followed by Evelyn, and last was Ann. Gordon was very careful not to tell her the names, just the number of each piece of paper. He had only marginal trust in Mrs Thomas but felt this was the fairest way to decide the order for each of the three women.

'What's this all about, Gordon?' Mrs Thomas was very suspicious.

'Oh, it's just a difficult decision I have to make,' he said vaguely, and stuttered, 'I wanted to make it a random choice. I'll let you know in good time.'

'You should try doing the lottery,' she said.

Try doing the lottery, mused Gordon. That's what his parents had done and, despite giving away the bulk of it, he was still in this predicament. 'By the way, Mrs Thomas, I'm going away for a while. Could you look after my cat please?'

'Yes, no problem. You go and enjoy yourself. Is it a cruise? You could meet some nice women on a cruise.'

'No, it's not a cruise,' replied Gordon. 'It's more exciting than that. I'll tell you all about it one day,' hoping in his heart of hearts that Mrs Thomas' curiosity would evaporate over the time he planned to spend on Le Treviot.

Emails were duly sent to the three ladies, who all responded enthusiastically. Joy agreed to 3rd-10th June; Evelyn, to 12th-19th June and Ann 22nd-29th. The days in between would enable Gordon to evaluate the situation and replenish his stores from Ile St Honorat.

It was only now that the real task began, and over the next couple of days Gordon purchased a tent, a sleeping bag, a cooking stove, camping gas, cutlery and all the things needed to make his stays – and those of his three different companions – comfortable.

In the end he was amazed at how much he had accumulated. He found a company willing to crate it up and deliver it to the hotel on Ile St Honorat. He then emailed

François with a request that Gustof would take the crates to Le Treviot and store them in the house.

Four days later he flew to Nice, took the ferry on to Ile St Honorat and was soon enjoying the hospitality of M le Patron. The next day Gustof was waiting at the quay as usual, and before long Gordon was on his island.

My Island, he thought, My Very Own Island. He did not have long to muse before tackling the enormous task of breaking open the crates and sorting out where everything was to go.

Gustof, who was very happy with the handsome sum of money Gordon had paid him, was curious. 'Is Monsieur planning to live here permanently?' he asked. With the thought of the stories of haunting in his mind, he was more than a little worried about his passenger. Two days back in the early spring was one thing, but now he looked as though he was here permanently!

'It's OK Gustof, I shall have some company next week. I am meeting her at the airport on Friday evening.'

'Her! Her!' Gustof could hardly contain himself. This Englishman is a cunning one to be sure, he thought. Gustof was interrupted in his curiosity by Gordon asking him to be there on Friday at 11am.

'OK.' Gustof was fine with that, and he chugged back to Ile St Honorat. That would give Gordon enough time to pick up his hire car to greet Joy off the 2.30pm arrival at the airport.

Gordon had noted that Joy was the most independent of the trio, had very few close relatives, mainly cousins, and lived a life that was slightly austere. Nevertheless, he found she had a ready wit and a beguiling smile. He wondered why she did not have a man in her life. Never mind, he thought. It was not for him to enquire into the pasts of the three, only to ascertain their suitability for the unusual adventure.

Joy's flight arrived on time and soon they were speeding

down the A8 to catch the ferry to Ile St Honorat and to the hotel where François was waiting to greet them. 'So this is the lady,' he exclaimed, kissing her audibly on each cheek, as was the local custom. When Joy had gone to the loo, Gordon explained they would only be on the island for one week.

'Enough to enjoy the sunshine and a little romance, hey?'

'No, it's not like that,' Gordon assured him. 'It's more a social experiment.'

'Social experiment! I don't understand you British people.' François had never heard of such a thing. 'They may practise that in Paris or London, but not here in the Med! I'll drink to your social experiment,' he continued, producing three glasses and a bottle of Vermouth. They hastily drained their glasses and Gustof was at the door, sweating profusely as he had been manhandling gas bottles which Gordon needed for the freezer, as well as solar panels to provide lighting for the cottage. Soon, with the boat loaded, they set off for Le Treviot.

Joy's eyes grew wider, but her heart missed a beat or two – what indeed had she let herself in for? Joy, the super-confident woman, a self-employed financial advisor, who could take time out if she wanted to?!

Luggage was landed and hauled up to the cottage. Gordon had indeed worked hard to make the place more habitable and had pitched his super tent in the lea by the back wall. 'I insist you sleep in the cottage,' he said to Joy. 'I'm very happy in the tent.'

Joy, who had had more than her fair share of suspicion all along, agreed demurely, in a way that ran contrary to her nature. She had brought her mobile phone, even though she knew there wouldn't be a signal on the island. Anyway, who was there to ring? She was hoping that the trip was going to be a cure, or at least partial cure, to her loneliness.

The next morning Gustof arrived with a dinghy and a good deal of excellent fishing gear. It was not long before Gordon and Joy put it all to use and a goodly catch of fish came ashore. Joy showed herself to be a skilled sailor while Gordon somehow managed the fishing gear.

All too soon Joy's week came to an end, and they were at the airport. 'You said we should treat it as a brother/sister relationship, and so it proved to be,' were Joy's farewell words, showing little emotion as she went into the departure lounge.

Gordon now had little more than 24 hours to prepare for the arrival of Evelyn. Back in Ile St Honorat he purchased new stocks of food and supplies and arranged for Gustof to take them to Le Treviot the next day. He then stayed overnight at the hotel before going to greet Evelyn at the airport.

Evelyn, Gordon soon discovered, was a very different person to Joy. Very warm-hearted and outgoing, she wanted to know why Gordon insisted on sleeping in his tent. 'There is plenty of space in the other room,' she commented. 'I won't disturb you.'

So Gordon complied. Evelyn was someone many found it hard, but not impossible, to say no to.

Their days were spent swimming, sailing and fishing, and early one morning Gordon took the shotgun Gustof had lent him and bagged a couple of rabbits. Neither of them fancied paunching or skinning them, but somehow they managed it and cooked the meat over an open fire. After they had eaten and washed the meal down with a couple of glasses of wine, Evelyn said, 'Look, it's a full moon. Let's go for a swim. We don't need to bother about costumes. After all, we're the only ones here.'

Soon they were enjoying the warm moonlit waters. As they came to the surface Evelyn grasped him tightly and kissed him passionately. With some effort he pushed her away. He might be trying to recreate his social experiment as a second Garden of Eden, but not like this! However, they agreed that clothes were optional and they resumed a more or less companionable relationship.

One day as they were sunbathing on the beach they saw a passing motor yacht, and the sun caught a reflection on a small piece of glass. Gordon thought no more of it until he was bidding farewell to Evelyn at the airport. His eye caught a headline on the news stand – 'Le Love Nest Anglais' – alongside photos of himself and Evelyn naked on the beach on his island. He could not believe his eyes!

This led to an immediate change of plans. He duly met Ann at the airport, partly explained the situation and, with Ann in tears, put her on the next flight home. He spoke to François at the hotel to ask Gustof to collect everything from the island and dispose of it. Then he contacted a local immobilier to sell Le Treviot and caught the next available flight home. It was all very sad.

He got home and checked his answerphone to discover a message and from Evelyn saying she hoped that they would be able to spend three long months together on Le Treviot.

A scratching noise at the door roused him and his cat pushed her way in to the bedroom. He woke up and realised his long dream was over, for it had all been just that – a dream!

Aunt Daisy's legacy

Aunt Daisy did not really enjoy the single life. She was not exactly a man-hater, but she had suffered so many disappointing relationships that, in the end, she felt she only wanted her own company.

Oh yes, her church was something of a lifeline but she felt that she could not reach out to others; she thought they shunned her. This was not exactly true, but it was her perception.

Then Jeffrey's grandmother died of cancer. Jeffrey was seven and he was taken to see her in hospital. It was a life-changing experience as he was very close to his grandma.

'Hospitals stink,' he shouted. 'They smell all funny and people die in them.'

'No they don't, Jeffrey, they make people better,' said his mother.

He was not convinced. 'Grandma's dying, isn't she?' he blurted out, impervious to his mother's comforting arm around him. He was aware of death as his beloved Old English Sheepdog had caught himself on barbed wire some weeks earlier and somehow poison had got into the wound. He was an only child and he loved the countryside – especially his pets, although some of them seemed to be dying. But Grandma was different.

Her funeral took place in the local parish church. Jeffrey was not allowed to go. Instead he played in the garden with his cousins while a neighbour kept watch. The tea afterwards was great. Yes, he did miss Grandma, but the food was good.

'Who's going to look after Granddad now he's on his own?'

It was the question of the hour for everyone in the village, and not least for the immediate family. Granddad thought he was quite capable of looking after himself, but he wasn't really. Aunt Freda, who lived some distance away, contributed in a loud voice, 'I know the Lord will care for him.'

'True,' said Jeffrey's mum, 'but who'll do his washing and cleaning?'

Everyone seemed to have an opinion, the consensus of which was that no one wanted to see Granddad on his own but nobody was willing to take on the role of his housekeeper.

'I'll do it,' said a quiet little voice. 'I can give up the tenancy of my flat in Guildford and come and live here. I don't particularly like country life, but I dare say I'll get used to it.'

So it was agreed. Jeffrey's father, who was away from home for much of the time and had only come back for his mother's funeral, said he would arrange everything, including talking his father into being looked after by Daisy, whom he neither liked nor disliked.

Granddad protested for a while, but eventually agreed it was for the best. So the date was set for Daisy to move into Granddad's cottage, which was sufficiently large for them to have separate accommodation.

The arrangement worked very well at first. Granddad was a proud man. In his earlier days he had been a valet in a ducal home, and he felt some of the more menial tasks around the home were not really for him. He loved his garden, though, and there was no shortage of fruit and vegetables.

However, when Jeffrey's father returned from his latest overseas trip he attempted to visit his father but was met at the door by Daisy saying his father was out and that he could not come in. Strange, he thought. Daisy's attitude certainly seemed to have changed in four months. Jeffrey and his mother had been visiting once or twice every week and Jeffrey loved sitting on Granddad's knee while Granddad told him stories of the old days, especially of what he called 'the big house'. Strangely, Aunt Daisy was always somewhere else when they called, perhaps shopping or in the garden. Jeffrey, being a child, did not know what was going on, but he sensed something of an 'atmosphere'.

Jeffrey's mother felt increasingly that they were intruding on Daisy's new empire. It became all the more obvious when Daisy became a vegan (Jeffrey had no idea what that was) and tried to impose her views on Granddad. His reaction was thoughtful but robust. 'If that's what she believes that's all right for her, but I still like my pork chops.'

'You'd better come for Sunday lunch each week,' was his daughter-in-law's response. Daisy had for some time imposed a 'no cooking' rule on Sundays, along with no TV or radio, so Granddad's regime on Sunday became to go to church separately from Daisy and go back to his daughter-in-law's for lunch.

Each time Jeffrey's father came home he found considerable changes surrounding his father. On the one hand they were grateful to Daisy for her care – the house was spotless, her financial arrangements were clear and transparent and Daisy herself seemed happy enough in her way. People at church thought she was wonderful – sacrificial even – in caring for Granddad. Others thought his daughter-in-law should have taken on the role, forgetting that she had a part-time job and her own house and garden to care for, let alone Lucky the dog and the two stray cats, Marco and Minerva, they had suddenly acquired.

The situation gradually deteriorated and Granddad's neighbours became a little suspicious. People at the church became divided over Daisy; one even suspected her of lining her own pockets at Granddad's expense, though such views were not verbally expressed.

Twelve months later, when Jeffrey's father came home on extended leave (with many a story to relate to his son), things came to a head. Jeffrey's father went to see Granddad and again was refused entry. Jeffrey's father was not one to lose his temper easily, but this was outrageous. 'Where is my Dad?' he demanded of Daisy.

'He's in the bath,' she replied.

'Daisy, I don't think that's true,' said Jeffrey's father, trying hard to suppress his feelings.

'Are you accusing me of lying?' she asked. 'Well, you can't see him and that's that.' With those words she closed the door.

Jeffrey's father hammered on the door to no avail. He looked in every available window and searched the garden and orchard but could find no sign of his father. He reluctantly retraced his steps home, almost on the verge of tears. When he arrived home, Jeffrey's mother asked, 'What's wrong?'

He quickly answered, 'Let's get indoors. Where's Jeffrey?'

She replied, 'Playing with friends up the road.'

Later that day Jeffrey could hear raised voices through the bedroom wall. 'What are we going to do? Where's my dad? I'm due to go back to India soon, and I haven't even been allowed to see my own father!'

Jeffrey could not understand what was happening. They were not arguing but they were clearly distressed. He knocked on his parents' door. 'Can I help?' he asked, with all the maturity that his seven and three-quarter years allowed.

'Sorry, son, this is a grown-ups' problem,' said his dad.

Jeffrey thought, I don't want to be grown up if I have problems like that.

As time went on, the situation deteriorated and Jeffrey was puzzled as to why he did not see his granddad whom he loved so much.

Then one day Daisy knocked at Jeffrey's parents' door.

When his mother opened it Daisy said coldly, 'I'm sorry to say that your father-in-law has passed away. I'm arranging the funeral.'

'Have you told my husband?' asked his mother.

'No, I'll leave you to do that,' with which words Daisy turned on her heel and left.

The vicar said some appropriate words at the funeral as a tribute to Jeffrey's granddad but the atmosphere was, to say the least, rather tense, especially when the Rev Gareth Tayler-Smyth said, 'We must all appreciate the sacrifice that Daisy has made over the past years in looking after her uncle.'

Following the burial in the churchyard the family and friends gathered in the church hall for cups of tea and biscuits (very plain ones), which Daisy made sure everyone knew she was paying for.

Jeffrey's family tried to keep a safe distance, which was not easy in the small hall, while many others crowded around Daisy, offering her comfort. One large gentleman insisted on quoting Bible verses and praying very audibly for Daisy. For the first time on that sad day Daisy's and Jeffrey's father's eyes met as they said their cool goodbyes.

'Mr Fortescue of Fortescue & Fortescue is coming to the house to read the will, so you might care to come,' said Daisy icily.

Knowing what was in the will his father had drawn up five years ago, Jeffrey's father made the excuse that he had to get back to Jeffrey before going back to the office to a job he didn't much care for but which paid quite well, although his importance was less than he imagined.

As they drove home he said casually to his wife, 'It's all very strange. I'm sure Dad's will was drawn up by Blake & Coldwell, not Fortescue & Fortescue. Never mind, I know he left the house and the bulk of his estate to me, with small legacies to Jeffrey, the church and Daisy.' With that they arrived home and he spent some time with Jeffrey, answering the curious boy's questions about the funeral and what happens to us when we die, and thanked the friend who had looked after him.

A week or so later Jeffrey's father remarked that Daisy would no doubt soon be wanting to go back to Guildford, and the empty property could be placed on the market for sale, adding that it should fetch a decent sum. Eventually the inaction and silence made Jeffrey's father ring Blake & Coldwell to fix an appointment.

He arranged to take time off work to see the senior partner, Mr Eustace Blake. Now Mr Blake (nobody, not even his somewhat downtrodden wife, ever called him Eustace) was every inch a solicitor of the old school.

'I've called to see about my late father's will,' was Jeffrey's dad's opening statement.

'Just a moment,' said Mr Blake, 'and I'll ask my secretary to retrieve the file.' It was eventually produced. Mr Blake opened it: it was empty – empty except for a typed note.

> The last Will and Testament of ....
> was removed from this file and handed to Mr Armstrong on .... as he is intending to replace it with another to be drawn up by and lodged with Fortescue & Fortescue of Granary Chambers.

The note had been signed by Jeffrey's grandfather and countersigned by Eustace Blake. The word 'shock' was probably an understatement of how Jeffrey's father felt at this news. He noted the date of the memo, said a polite goodbye and rang Fortescue & Fortescue, who arranged for him to see their senior partner an hour later.

'I know this will be hurtful to you,' Mr Fortescue was a kind soul who hated giving bad news, 'but your father left everything to your cousin Daisy in gratitude for her care for him over the past two and a half years since your mother died.' Jeffrey's father's dreams of a new conservatory and a private education for his son evaporated like the morning mist.

How could he? How could she? came to mind, followed by, The cunning old vixen, although Daisy was five years younger than Jeffrey's father.

'I'll think about contesting this will,' was his paltry remark as he left to go home, poorer, he thought, than when his father was alive.

The tension between Jeffrey's parents increased somewhat over the following weeks. Late at night, Jeffrey would hear words such as 'contesting the will' and 'greedy old bat', which he didn't understand, as the only old bat he knew was his father's cricket bat with which he claimed to have scored many more runs than he ever actually did!

Jeffrey's father consulted various friends as to what action to take, and even asked the vicar, who suggested they pray about it and said politely that kind Daisy had indeed left her home to look after the old gentleman for two and a half years. Jeffrey's father snorted, 'Rev Tayler-Smyth, I am the son who has been done out of his just inheritance. It's no wonder I don't come to *your* church. They're all a bunch of hypocrites!'

We could do with a few more, was the unspoken thought of Rev Tayler-Smyth as he made his farewell.

Time moved on. In the end the will was not contested, not least because Jeffrey's father did not want his name splashed across the press or to have to face Daisy in court. Promotion was in the offing and he did not want to do anything to jeopardise his chances.

Jeffrey grew up, gained a degree in computing and began

work in an engineering firm. In due time he met, fell in love with and married Jill, whom he had vaguely known as a boy.

One day they were shocked to hear from his mother that his father was seriously ill. They rushed to the hospital, where it was obvious his beloved Dad was dying. They exchanged a number of father and son pleasantries, and eventually Jeffrey plucked up the courage to say, 'Dad, I think you and I know what the situation is er... er...'

'Go on, son,' replied his dad weakly.

'Dad, you remember Aunt Daisy?'

'Can't forget her, even now. What a hypocrite!' shouted his father so loudly that all the other patients heard, and the staff nurse rushed to see what was wrong.

'Dad, don't waste your breath. I... I just wondered if there is anything I can do so that you can be reconciled?'

His father, exhausted by his outburst, whispered, 'You could go and try to see her but...' again raising his voice, '... it won't do any good, and I don't want you emotionally scarred as I have been.'

With that effort, he slipped back into an unconscious state, from which he never recovered.

Tears flowed down Jeffrey and Jill's faces. They were tears of sadness at having to say farewell to his beloved father, but more so because his father had never been reconciled to his cousin. Jeffrey's thoughts strayed somewhat, and he confided in Jill, 'Perhaps being a computer manager isn't really what I want to do.'

Many, many years later, Jeffrey found himself working in a hostel for homeless young men. It didn't pay very well but, as a Christian, he felt called to serve this way.

One day, a letter arrived for him with the branding 'Fortescue & Fortescue'. Whatever can it be? he wondered, as he tore open the envelope.

'Dear Mr Armstrong,' it read. 'Under the terms of the will of the late Daisy Basker, the sum of £10,000 is bequeathed to you.'

In a separate envelope there was a note in Daisy's handwriting:

Dear Jeffrey,
Just to let you know I too have a conscience. I admire the work you are doing amongst the homeless.
Love Daisy (alias 'stupid old bat')

One of our kettles is missing
or
The prodigal dog

Dave and Margaret settled down to their new married life. There were a lot of things to be sorted out, both emotionally and practically. The local charity shops welcomed a vast amount of spare furniture and other household items. Kettle the dog did not know quite what to make of it. He was puzzled, but he enjoyed his walks with Dave, who insisted on taking him out twice a day.

They had spent their brief honeymoon in France on the Ile St Honorat, having flown to Nice before going on there. They had chosen a comfortable, clean hotel near the harbour, and the proprietor, François, made them very welcome. Margaret had never flown before; indeed, this was her first ever foreign trip. They were extremely happy in each other's company.

They became curious about another island that they saw shining in the morning sunlight. François informed them it was called Le Treviot and that no one ever went there, few had ever lived there – at least, not now – and there was a legend that it is haunted.

'Can we go over to see it?' pleaded Margaret, her new-found sense of adventure knowing no bounds.

'Gustof at the far end of the harbour has a boat. Ask him and he might take you,' was François' reply. So it was arranged. At 9am the next morning Gustof was waiting with his outboard chugging, and soon they were landing on Le Treviot, arranging with him to collect them at 6pm. They had taken packed lunches, a filled thermos flask, lots of water, sun cream and all the necessary paraphernalia for a day in the sun.

'Let's go and explore first,' said Margaret. They worked their way all around the shoreline. Margaret very much appreciated the wildlife, especially the flocks of oystercatchers and a sanderling or two. She thought how much she would like to report to her local natural history group when they returned about the gannets diving for fish just offshore. She had never given a talk to the club. In fact, despite winning a prestigious award, she had never been invited to! Now perhaps, with her new confidence since her marriage to Dave, she could at least offer. So out came her camera and video camera to record all the wonderful world of this deserted island.

The sea looked so inviting. 'No need for clothes!' cried Margaret, stripping off and running into the briny. Indeed, they were to have as private a day as anybody could wish for.

'If people at church could see us now,' exclaimed Dave.

'Well they can't, and we won't tell,' responded Margaret.

Dave pulled her close to him, saying, 'You are now my Naturist of the Year.'

Back home, Kettle was very confused. He had grown used to Dave, but now he had gone to stay with Freda and Gavin, two younger, fairly new members of the church. They were kind and walked him a lot; as Gavin was a shift-worker most walks were in the morning.

One day Kettle discovered a hole in the fence. His doggy mind seemed to suggest to him that this might be interesting to explore. Before long he was back at his old haunts. He barked at the front door but neither Margaret nor Dave responded.

So off he went, down the lane, under the stile, across the field, all familiar territory, until he got to Stragglers Lane. All of a sudden there was a screech of brakes and a fast four-by-four just missed him.

Recovering, he trotted on, stopping for a drink at a place the humans called St Michael's Well. He heard a familiar sound behind him. It was the clip-clop of the hooves of Samson out for his daily ride. 'Hello,' said the rider. 'Are you a little dog lost?'

Now Kettle had no fear of horses even though they were a lot bigger than he was. He also had no idea what 'lost' meant. All he knew was that he was hungry and this person seemed friendly.

Angela, Samson's rider, saw a car coming, so she flagged it down and explained the situation to the driver and asked for his help to lift Kettle onto Samson's back so she could take him home.

'I'm not strong enough to lift the dog up that high,' replied the elderly driver. Samson was a horse who lived up to his biblical name in stature – he was very tall and well built. But they had better luck when Steve, a local farmer who happened to be passing on his tractor, stopped to help. Before long, Kettle was settled comfortably with Angela on Samson's back and retracing the steps he had earlier taken down the road. Angela was surprised at how happy he seemed to be, though she did find it hard to hold on to him when Sir Marcus Rigby hooted at them as he tried to pass in the narrow lane in his Rolls Royce.

Eventually the two and a half miles or so were retraced and, to Kettle's surprise, Freda and Gavin were walking along the road, looking for him.

'Thank goodness you've been found,' cried Freda, carrying the tired little dog back home.

Dave and Margaret flew home after a wonderful holiday, discussing as they travelled the marvellous day they had spent on Le Treviot. 'I don't think it's haunted,' commented Margaret as their plane was landing.

'Neither do I,' said Dave, but neither was 100 per cent convinced.

On arriving home they duly unpacked. 'Shall we eat first or collect Kettle?' asked Margaret.

'Oh, let's collect Kettle,' was Dave's enthusiastic reply.

It was a good half mile to Freda and Gavin's home. Kettle greeted them with joyful barking – he was absolutely delighted. He had never been away from Margaret in all his 14 years, and the week had seemed like a lifetime to him. His thoughts must have been that now they had returned, he would soon be in his own home again.

Freda and Gavin were soon recounting Kettle's adventure and his rescue by Angela and Samson.

'What a story,' said Margaret.

'Praise the Lord,' whispered Dave under his breath, not wishing to embarrass the couple, kind as they were, as he did not know whether they – as yet – shared his Christian beliefs.

Back home, Kettle was soon checking things out and getting back to what he saw as normal.

'Welcome home, prodigal dog,' said Dave loudly. 'Are we going to kill the fatted calf?'

'No,' said Margaret firmly, 'but I have got some fillet steak, and I guess he can have a tiny piece!'

So you were not 'done' as a child?

Freya was walking past St Agatha's one Sunday morning on her way to the supermarket when she noticed a large crowd emerging from the church, all dressed very smartly. It must be a christening, she thought. They seem to have a lot there; it's an attractive church and that new young vicar seems to be pulling them in.

However, her musings were cut short by her need to dig out her shopping list as she navigated her way past crowds of shoppers, not dressed in their Sunday best but nevertheless out to enjoy themselves. How strange Sundays are these days, she thought – a full church (if only briefly) next to a full supermarket.

A few days later Freya was in town again, this time to pick up one or two bits and pieces at her local market, and to wander round the stalls. She liked it better than the supermarket as it was friendlier. Sam, who ran the fruit and veg stall, always greeted her with a smile. Today his smile seemed just a bit brighter and wider than usual. Since her painful divorce some three years ago she had tried hard to avoid male company.

'Go and get yourself another fella,' had been the advice of her sister Louise. 'You're still attractive enough to pull the blokes.' Melvin in the office had taken her out for a drink a couple of times, but nothing had come of it. She had felt very let down by Mac, her former husband, and although the financial arrangements had been reasonably equitable she had felt something of a failure. And now here was Sam beaming at her.

'I… I'll have… some carrots and some peas,' was all she

could stammer.

'No problem,' he replied. 'Dad and I grew them ourselves; they're what you might call "organic".'

Freya paid up and was just about to turn away when her curiosity got the better of her. She blurted out, 'What makes you so cheerful today?'

Sam looked round, making sure no customers were waiting to be served – in his trade you didn't want to miss a sale – and then replied, 'Well, last Sunday I got baptised. It was great! The effect hasn't rubbed off yet, and I don't suppose it ever will.'

'What?!' exploded Freya. 'The vicar picked you up and splashed you with water?!'

'No,' shouted Sam as he tried to make himself heard above the sounds of the market and the passing traffic. 'I was dunked in water. They have a pool in the church – it's called a baptistery. I was never done as a kid, and now I'm a committed Christian it seemed the right thing to do.'

'I wasn't "done" as a kid either,' Freya said. By this time a queue of potential customers was lining up and some were showing signs of impatience.

'Why don't you come back next week, and when we close we can talk about it?' were Sam's parting words.

'Talk about what?' asked the queen of the town's gossips. 'His fruit and veg are OK but he won't chat me up like that!'

'Some chance,' thought Agnes, a fellow gossip.

A week later, as the stalls were being packed away, Freya rather shyly appeared at Sam's stall. She had little time for religion as she saw it. It seemed hypocritical and over-organised. Mac had wanted to get married in church as he thought it was the 'proper thing to do', but she preferred the registry office, and that is where they went.

However, when it came to the reception it was a different matter. Little was spared, in spite of Freya's father moaning about the cost, to everyone's embarrassment, and he made sure in his speech that they all knew how much he had spent. Some people got very drunk and fireworks were let off prematurely.

The next day Freya and Mac woke up with massive hangovers, which in some ways were to last for the entire 14 years of their married life – a marriage which for the last ten years was really in name only. Armed neutrality was perhaps a better description of how it had been most of the time. Sex was a forgotten dream, and children were other people's problems. Mac eventually sought the company of Lucy, a receptionist at work, and Freya was left bemoaning her lot.

'Should never have married 'im,' was her father's somewhat less than constructive comment.

Freya helped Sam pack up his trestle tables and packed the unsold goods into his van parked nearby. 'Here, have a big bunch of grapes to say thanks for your help. Didn't grow them myself but they do taste good,' said Sam with a broad smile. 'Cup of tea?'

'Thank you,' replied Freya, who rarely received presents of any sort, even for her birthday or Christmas.

Once they were settled at a side table in the Corner Café, Sam began to explain to Freya some of the reasons for his newfound happiness, which at this point in time seemed to be somewhat overflowing.

Despite her scorn for her idea of religion, Freya began to sit up and take notice of what he was saying, and she realised that this was the first time she had felt comfortable in male company for some long while.

Sam's explanation was simple and direct. He had come across a group of teenagers from a local church. He had been very suspicious of them at first as he had suffered at the hands of gangs before, one group even going so far as to turn over his vegetable stall. Somehow, though, these people seemed different.

'"Hi," said a tall guy with a dirty shirt, "can we buy some of your apples?" and then he added, "We're from St Agatha's just down the road; just out to bring a smile or two to people's faces." Well,' said Sam, 'before I knew where I was, I was going to St Agatha's the following Sunday morning. I had to make my excuses to the football team. Since my nasty accident two years ago I can't play any more but I run the line for the pub team. St Agatha's is a different kind of church,' he continued. 'People are welcoming and friendly.' Sam just stopped himself from adding, 'Not like the one up the road.'

'The third time I went (and by this time the pub team were getting cross with me), I decided the Christian life was really the only one worth living. I told the minister about it. Of course there were lots of questions on both sides but, to cut a long story short, I made a public, or semi-public, commitment, and here I am – a new man!'

'All very interesting,' said Freya, trying not to sound like her sarcastic father. 'I've never been done.' Freya, who hated water except in tea and who had never bothered to learn to swim, was only mildly curious.

Later that night Freya lay awake. She rarely slept well these days, and tonight was no exception. A nagging thought kept coming to her brain. What if Sam's right? What makes him so happy? Why am I so miserable? Perhaps I should try praying. So she actually got out of bed and on to her knees – something she had never done before – but nothing happened. This God, if there is one, didn't seem to answer prayers. With that she got back into bed and, for the first time in months, slept soundly.

For the next few weeks Freya avoided the market and bought her fruit and vegetables in the supermarket. Going there on Sunday mornings meant there was no real chance of meeting Sam as he would be in church. But still the questions haunted her – Why? Why? Why?

There had been plenty of questions in her life. Why did she marry Mac? Why did they not have any children? Why did he leave her?

'Peace, woman,' said the tall, strange man, dressed in some kind of eastern garb with a greying ponytail trailing down his back. 'Peace,' he repeated in a somewhat ritualistic way.

'P-p-p-peace,' stammered Freya, wondering what on earth this guy was doing in the precincts of the supermarket. A leaflet was thrust into her unwilling hand. It read, 'Do you want peace in your life?'

You bet I do, thought Freya, and she read on. 'Come to the Sharma Temple in Dove Street at 7.30pm each Saturday.'

So, rather reluctantly but with great curiosity, that is where Freya found herself the following Saturday evening. She had tried ringing one or two acquaintances (she could not stretch to calling them friends) but they all were busy that night, so she had rather timidly made it alone. The smell of incense hit her as soon as she walked through the door. The room, bedecked in flowers, looked vaguely 'churchy' – it had at one time been a Masonic hall, and since then had been used by all sorts of groups, although none for very long owing mainly to the high maintenance costs and rents.

Now it was the Sharma Temple, and there, sitting cross-legged in the middle of the room, was the hippy type she had encountered outside the supermarket. He looked serene as well as a bit surreal. There were about 20 other people sitting or lying around the hall; some even appeared to be asleep.

'Peace, sister,' said the ponytailed one.

'P-p-p-p-eace,' Freya stammered in reply.

'It is "Peace, brother",' was the reply in a faintly corrective voice. The voice became stronger, louder and more demanding. 'Brothers and sisters, we come in peace.' There was a general murmuring around the gathering. 'If we want peace,' he boomed, 'we must placate the gods.'

As if by magic, two things happened at once: a burst of music, seemingly from hidden harpists, flooded the room, and a quartet of scantily dressed young women appeared from behind a screen. The lights dimmed and the music increased in volume, and the four girls began a form of hypnotic dance.

'I can't cope with this,' thought Freya. 'What does it all mean?'

After some moments the music faded and a spotlight beamed on the ponytailed 'master'. He intoned, 'If there is anyone here who longs, who craves, for peace in their life, who has for years sought real peace, who has tried other religions and found them wanting...'

That's not me, thought Freya. I haven't tried any religion until now, except perhaps this one, whatever it is. Nevertheless she carried on listening in rapt attention, for she desperately wanted something in her life. But peace at any price? She did not know.

The 'master' continued, 'If this is your desire and you know your heart, come with me to the Shalom Temple behind me.' Again, as if by magic, the two gold and purple curtains behind a throne parted to reveal a glass door with a blazing light shining through it. The music started again, this time much more softly and seductively. Freya felt his eyes burning through her and she got to her feet (she realised she had been sitting cross-legged on the floor all evening) and took a step forward. The hypnotic trance was beginning to overwhelm her. She felt everyone looking at her, urging her on to find the peace that lay behind the glass door.

The 'master' was standing with his arms outstretched toward her in a welcoming posture. 'Come and find peace,' he boomed, enunciating the word 'peace' in such a way that it seemed an all-embracing invitation that could not be resisted.

Freya returned his gaze and their eyes met as though they

were two lovers looking at each other. She looked at the glass door again and then around the room. No one else was moving, other than gently swaying, and all eyes were firmly fixed on her, waiting for her decision. Suddenly she screamed and began to run, not towards the glass door but for the exit, which she hit with all her might. The four scantily dressed girls quickly followed and almost caught her. Outside the cold air hit her and the four girls drew back and did not follow.

Freya could not get home soon enough. She collapsed into bed and fell asleep, albeit disturbed by nightmarish dreams of the evening's experiences.

It was several weeks since she had been to the market as she was still trying to avoid Sam. She was in the queue at the post office when she noticed a tall, handsome man standing behind her. It was quite a long wait so she whiled away the time by looking at the notices on display. 'You are never too old to learn to swim,' said one. Having noticed her reading it, the tall man asked, 'Are you interested in swimming?'

'No, no not really. I hate water,' Freya replied.

'That's a pity. I love swimming. I'm a lifeguard at the local pool and I teach people twice a week. There's nothing to be scared of.' Freya was hoping that either the queue would move rapidly forward or the ground would open and swallow her up. Neither happened. 'Why not come along on Sunday morning? The first session is free and it would be a pleasure to teach you.'

Just then the queue did move forward as the old gent who could not make up his mind whether he was paying in or taking out, or how many second-class stamps he wanted, was sorted out and Freya got to the counter.

Later that day she thought, why is everybody inviting me to things? First of all it was Smiley Sam, then the ponytailed 'master,' now it was this lifeguard. Am I the flavour of the month or something?

For the next couple of days the invitation to the pool kept ringing around her confused brain. No, I'm not going on Sunday morning, she thought, and made up her mind. But he is very handsome, though. I can almost feel his strong arms holding me up, conquering my fear, she dreamed. Her distaste for men had certainly hardened after her experience in the 'temple' but, in some ways, this lifeguard was someone a bit like Sam: kind, thoughtful and certainly better looking.

All through Saturday she was restless and fidgety as she wrestled with the idea of going to the swimming lessons at the nearby pool. I'll go. No I won't go. But he is nice and it would be a pity to let him down, and it is free. Anyway, I haven't got a cossy so that settles it. I'll do something else tomorrow.

Suddenly the phone rang. Who could that be on a Saturday evening? Some prankster, no doubt. 'Hello?' she answered timidly.

'Hello.' It was a man's voice, sounding gentle and thoughtful. 'I hope you don't mind me ringing. I tracked you down through my friend, Sam, at the market stall. I'm Craven. You may remember we met in the post office queue.'

Freya was gobsmacked and could not answer.

'Freya? Freya, are you still there?' His voice sounded quite urgent. 'Are you going to come to the lesson tomorrow?'

Freya could only stammer a hesitant 'Yes.'

'You don't sound too sure.'

'Well, I haven't got a cossy.'

'No problem,' he replied.

So, after a sleepless night, Freya found herself at the local swimming pool, and there was Craven, looking very sporty in his emerald green tracksuit, every inch a lifeguard. There were seven other people there: two older men, three giggly teenage girls and two women in their late thirties who were obviously friends. Whether it was the promise of a free lesson or the encouragement of someone like Craven who had brought them along, no one could tell.

'See Vicky in reception. She'll fix you up with a costume,' Craven said to her.

Freya changed and admired herself in the mirror. Not bad, if I say it myself, she thought. Her confidence, which had been at an all-time low, was thus boosted just a little.

Craven made them sit around on plastic chairs at the poolside. They were the sole users so there was no escaping. 'Just a few dos and don'ts and some safety instructions,' he said, before issuing them with arm bands and foam buoyancy aids.

'Now get in one at a time, please. You first, Freya.'

'Me?' she almost screamed. 'Me!'

'Yes please.'

So, very gingerly, she lowered herself into the water. It was lovely and warm and clean and the feeling was almost comforting. Craven, who had stripped off, was beside her in the water and she felt his arms underneath her as she lay back, now almost beginning to enjoy her first lesson. It was much nicer than she had dared hope. The two older men took it very seriously, the teenage girls thought it quite a laugh and didn't pay much attention except to ogle Craven, and the two friends chatted to each other.

After half an hour or so, all were quite happy with the experience. A few managed a stroke or two. Craven praised their courage and deemed the session a success. He encouraged them to sign up for the full course of ten sessions.

In the cafeteria they all sat round in a circle and more than a few compliments were flying around. One of the older men thought Freya had put in the most effort and was top of the class!

'Don't know about that,' spluttered Freya with due modesty,

'but I'll treat you to another cup of coffee.' However, soon they all made their excuses and left her alone with the handsome Craven.

Freya's courage was rising all the time. 'Craven, I hope you don't mind, but I'd like to ask you a few questions.'

'Fire away,' he replied.

'Well, how did you get the name Craven? It's unusual for a first name, isn't it?'

'Well, to cut a long story short, my parents died when I was very young and my grandparents adopted me and they gave me the name Craven. Granddad used to smoke a lot and his favourite was Craven A, so that's how I got my name. It's really John Craven Fellows, but I prefer Craven as it's unusual.'

Freya went further with her next question. 'Why are you a lifeguard?'

'Well, I enjoy swimming and, having passed various exams, I qualified two years ago.'

After some hesitation, Freya signed up for the Learn to Swim course, paid her money at reception, expressed her thanks to Craven and said a polite goodbye.

During the week she went shopping and bought herself a new costume which, in flaming red, looked – or so she thought – more glamorous than the one she had hired from the pool. The week went by and she saw nothing of Sam or Craven. The prospect of the session on Sunday morning haunted her not a little, but it was mitigated by the thought of seeing Craven and knowing that he would be there to help her should she falter in her attempts to doggy paddle with the buoyancy aid.

Sunday morning came and, despite further misgivings, she found herself at the pool with her new swimsuit, complete with goggles. She changed with a certain eagerness and joined the other 'debutantes'. She then waited to be summoned to the poolside.

Her courage began to fade when there was no sign of Craven. Instead there was an older man who introduced himself as Edwin.

'Where's Craven?' she asked, trying not to sound too agitated at his absence.

'Oh, he's at his church, St Agatha's. He only helps out when we're very short staffed.' Fortunately, no one noticed her countenance, but she felt totally let down. She coped with the session quite well, and even said to herself, 'I could, perhaps, enjoy this,' but more in doubt than optimism.

Back home, she pondered on the fact that the two men she had met recently somehow seemed different, and strangely they both went to St Agatha's. Perhaps she should try this religion lark, she thought, before dismissing the idea almost immediately. Her thoughts were in a muddle when the telephone rang. It did not take her long to discover it was Craven.

'Hi,' the voice said.

There was a long silence before she felt able to answer. She eventually managed a feeble 'Hi.'

'How's the swimming going?'

'OK.' Freya was now in monosyllabic mode.

'Are you still enjoying it?'

'Yes and no,' was all she could utter.

'Well, try to explain a bit,' was his sympathetic reply.

Freya, now a little more relaxed, said, 'Well, I did manage ten or twelve strokes on my own. Yes, I'm feeling a good deal more confident in the water now. No,' she almost shouted down the phone, 'you weren't there. I hear you were stuck at your rotten old church. I feel very let down.'

'Sorry about that,' replied Craven. 'As a committed Christian, Sunday worship is really my priority.'

'Well, you can stick your rotten Sunday worship,' and with that she slammed the phone down. Immediately she regretted her rudeness and tried to dial Craven's number, only to find it engaged. Her emotions were now in such a turmoil that she did not know what to do. The phone rang again, and she waited a long time before answering. Eventually she answered with a cautious 'Hello?'

It was indeed Craven and she was profuse in her apologies.

'Forget it,' was his quick response. 'Look, can I take you out for a meal? How about Thursday? I know a nice gastro-pub in Luke Street and I could explain things in a little more detail.'

'Well, OK,' she said. She was still very, very, cautious. 'But none of that religious stuff.'

'I'll pick you up about 7pm.'

Well, what a situation, was her first thought, after saying an almost tearful goodbye.

The four days until Thursday evening were filled with conflicting emotions. She had a history, as she saw it, of being let down by men. Her father, her ex-husband, she even included Sam, and now here was Craven seemingly trying to make amends.

Sleepless nights followed one after another, and more than once she thought about picking up the phone to cancel Thursday's meeting. Apart from the short time with Sam, she had been reluctant to trust herself to any man for a long while, but she thought maybe this one was different.

Thursday evening came and she put on her most attractive dress, something she had not worn for years. Amazingly, it fitted perfectly, but then she changed her mind and went back to something less daring and more conservative. What the hell, she thought, and just managed to change back again before the doorbell rang.

Craven stood there with a bunch of flowers in his hand. Her heart missed a beat – this man cares about me just a little, she thought as she invited him in and found a vase for the flowers.

The pub was crowded but, as Craven had booked a table, they were ushered into a cosy corner. 'What are you drinking?' he asked.

Freya did not know how to answer. 'Er, er, perhaps a glass of red wine,' she stammered. So Craven ordered a glass of Merlot and a glass of orange juice for himself.

'Do you not drink?' she enquired.

'Yes, I do,' he replied, 'but when I'm driving I'm very careful what I consume.' This man at least has a degree of responsibility, thought Freya.

They examined the menu and decided on their choices. 'No starter, thank you,' said Freya, asking for the steak pie as it was the cheapest option available, while Craven ordered a starter followed by a sirloin steak. She was amazed at his appetite. Part of the reason for ordering less than him wasn't that she was not hungry but that she felt she did not want to be under a great obligation to him.

The food duly arrived. 'Do you mind if I say grace?' said Craven.

This threw Freya. In front of all these people? she thought as she nodded and added a mumbled 'Amen' at the end. He's such a handsome chap, she thought, but he wants to bring religion into everything. Why can't he keep it locked up in the church?

An awkward silence descended, eventually broken by Freya wanting to know exactly what Craven had been doing at church on Sunday.

'I was involved in baptising an older couple,' he explained.

'I thought that was the vicar's job,' was her quick reply.

'Yes, it is, but several others help. It's a bit like teaching people to swim, only this time they drown. Oh, not literally,' he hastily added.

'I said keep off religion,' was Freya's emphatic response. 'Don't spoil our meal and our time together.' So again, an awkward silence descended. Freya was full of doubts and questions that she certainly did not want to express in public, and he was curious to know what it was that motivated this girl in life; she was becoming increasingly attractive in his eyes. He felt that, as yet, he did not know the real Freya.

'Thank you for a lovely meal.' Freya's understated gratitude belied the truth that it was ages since she had shared such good food and male company.

'I think I'd better get you home,' he said.

'I'll call a cab,' she responded.

'Oh no you won't. I'll take you,' Craven insisted.

'Well, OK,' she agreed weakly.

'Hi Freya. Who's the handsome bloke, then? You're a bit of a dark horse!' It was Justine from the office, half drunk on a night out with her friends. 'How did you pull this one?'

Freya, who had been the victim of confusing emotions all evening, was just about to burst into tears, when Craven stepped forward and saved the day. It's OK, it's an unfinished business meeting and we're just off on our separate ways.'

Justine, in her intoxicated state, could not get her head round the words 'unfinished business meeting' – not that she could get her head round much at that moment. She just stood there and, before she could utter anything approaching a coherent remark, Craven had swept Freya out of the door and into his car. Freya found it cramped in his Micra, so how he managed to squeeze himself into it was, she thought, a minor miracle.

Craven responded positively to Freya's invitation to a cup of coffee. She put the percolator on and then went to her bedroom and slipped into something more casual. She certainly found Craven attractive in spite of his religion, but wasn't sure whether she wanted to go as far as seducing him. Would it cap or spoil a lovely evening? She didn't know.

Craven had made the coffee and was surveying her

bookshelves. "Fraid it's mostly sci-fi and adult literature. Nothing classic like Dickens or Hardy,' she said apologetically.

'That's OK,' was Craven's response. 'Everybody's taste is different,' noting that what Freya called 'adult literature' was, at the very least, mildly pornographic. 'Freya, can I ask you something?'

'Ask away,' was her response, hoping for something romantically engaging from this tall, handsome man.

'Are you still thinking about being baptised, or "being done" as you put it?'

Craven saw the disappointment on Freya's face, who had by now moved closer to him on the settee.

Why bring religion into this lovely evening? she thought. Keep it in St Agatha's. But instead she stammered, 'Er, yes and no. Yes, I feel there is a gap, and no to this Christianity lark.'

'Well,' he replied, 'I'm afraid you can't have one without the other. Heavens, is that the time? I must be going!' And with that he gave Freya a quick kiss on the cheek, which was a lot less than she had been hoping for, and made his way to the door. 'Goodnight Freya. Thank you for making the evening so special.'

The next morning at the office, Justine, now sober, although bleary eyed, was quick to remark, 'Nice bloke you had there, Freya. Where did you get him from? What's he like in bed?'

'None of your business,' barked Freya and got down to work at her desk.

Back home that evening she dialled Craven's number, full of hesitation, and was relieved to get his answerphone. 'Freya here. Just to say thank you for the lovely evening. If... if... you've got any bumph on baptism, as you call it, can you drop it in? Just put it through the letter box. Don't call in, please.'

The following morning she was surprised to find an envelope on the doormat marked 'Freya'. Inside was an attractive-looking leaflet headed *So You Were Not Done As A Child?*

It explained, in simple language, what Christian baptism was about and that these days many people had not been baptised as infants, and how, in adulthood, they could indeed understand what it meant. There were three headings marked Believing, Behaving and Belonging which explained the need to trust in Christ, to live the Christian life and to belong to a church community. The author had added one or two verses from the Bible, but Freya did not think it was as 'heavy' as some religious material she had seen.

No to the believing bit, although she was becoming a sceptic about her agnosticism; yes to question two: I try to behave like a Christian – well, some of the time – and a definite no to the last one: she certainly did not want to belong to a church!

The weeks went by. Craven rang her from time to time. She finished her swimming lessons and could now swim some 20 yards, if she didn't get bored. She saw the cheery Sam at his market stall now and again, but otherwise life was pretty routine and dull. Then, one morning, she noticed that Justine was not at her desk as usual and thought, 'Well at least I don't have to put up with her sarcastic banter today.'

The next thing she knew, her supervisor called her into his office. What have I done now? she wondered.

'I don't really know how to put this,' he said. 'I have something to tell you: last night, Justine stepped into the road and was hit by a passing car. She died in hospital three hours later.'

Tears welled up in Freya's eyes. As much as she disliked Justine's barbs, she was in a way fond of her, and thought it was a horrible way to die.

'Take some time out if you wish,' said the supervisor sympathetically.

'I'll go into the rest room for a while,' replied Freya. Apart from a water cooler, a few books and some leaflets about health and safety and childcare, the rest room was empty. Then a bright red booklet caught her eye – it was labelled *So You Were Not Done as a Child?*

Freya was gobsmacked. 'I can't get away from him,' she thought.

To her surprise, Justine's funeral was at St Agatha's. The vicar took it beautifully, and one of her friends – now quite sober – paid a short tribute. Lots of people came from the office, and out of the corner of her eye Freya could see Sam and his wife, and Craven.

The vicar spoke about the shortness of life and the claims of Christ upon people's lives. Here we go again, thought Freya. He ended the service with an invitation to the church hall for refreshments. She turned round and there, prominently on the bookshelf, were copies of *So You Were Not Done as a Child?* Before she knew it Craven was standing there smiling at her, and she dissolved into tears.

Eventually she responded to the invitation to tea in the hall and when she, Sam and his wife, and Craven were seated, he managed to ask her, 'Did you read the red leaflet I popped through your letterbox?'

'Yes,' she replied. 'And the answers are no-ish, yes-ish, and no-ish.' The latter was a small advance in the complete rejection of church, the shift in her position being due to the sensitive way the vicar had taken the funeral and the friendly reception she had received at the church.

Craven was at a crossroads. He was certainly attracted to Freya. He could see she had retracted her opposition ever so slightly, but he was at a loss to know where to go next. He prayed inwardly for guidance, but none appeared to come.

Weeks later, Freya was at the market stall again, and found Sam smiling, as ever. 'Hello,' he chirped. 'What can I sell you today? Some lovely grapes?' Freya readily purchased grapes and some other fruit. As Sam was taking her cash with a polite 'Thank you,' he added, 'Got some news for you. Do you remember your colleague Justine who was killed, what was it, about three months ago?'

'Four months and two days,' replied Freya, 'and I don't need reminding. It was awful.' But she was curious enough to enquire what exactly the news was.

'Her brother, Tom, wants to be baptised at our church,' said Sam.

Freya was absolutely shocked, to say the least, for Tom had a reputation as a loud-mouthed, hard-drinking salesman who had, in fact, spent several short terms in prison.

'Why not come along on Sunday week and see what it's all about?'

'I might just...' was all Freya could reply, clutching her purchases tightly while trying not to squash the fruit. She tried not to look embarrassed as the queue behind her began to build up.

I suppose I could miss swimming for once, she mused as she walked home, and Craven would be there. She hadn't seen Craven for several weeks and was beginning to miss him.

Just after 10.30am she slipped into the church, hopefully unnoticed, during the first hymn. Some of Justine's family were in the front row with Tom, not in his salesman's outfit, but in a white suit looking more like a cricketer than an angel.

The service continued. Craven was preaching on baptism, saying it was a bit like learning to swim, but it is all about that word 'trust'. You have to trust the swimming instructor, and in baptism you have to show your trust in Jesus.

Phrases like, 'Do you repent of your sins?' (Freya hadn't a

clue what that meant) and 'Do you turn to Christ?' were responded to by Tom. Here come those religious bits, thought Freya, and then Tom was duly dunked under the water by the vicar, this time wearing swimming trunks.

After the service, Freya sought out Craven. 'Hello,' he said, holding out a cup of coffee. 'Thought you might just come. Did you enjoy the service?'

'Enjoy' did not seem to be the right word, thought Freya. 'Er, yes,' she mumbled. 'It was lovely. Has Tom really changed or is he going through a religious bit after his sister died? I've been told people get religion when a crisis occurs in their life. It's all emotions, you know.' Craven looked at her; the kindness in his eyes somewhat melted her responses, and she mumbled, 'No, I don't really think that's true.'

'Let's go and talk to Jordan Richards, our vicar,' he said.

'All right,' replied Freya, without any enthusiasm. Jordan had now changed and was looking a bit more 'vicarish'. Craven introduced Freya and explained how they had met up. Jordan already knew a good deal from parish gossip – that they were almost, but not quite, 'an item'.

Never at a loss for words, and obviously well briefed by Craven, Jordan said, 'I guess all this is a bit odd to you. Would you like to come and talk about baptism?'

'Er – yes,' said Freya, when she really meant no. The conversation continued a while, but before it ended Jordan had fixed a date for Freya to call round and see him.

So, one evening after work, without telling any of her colleagues, she found herself nervously ringing the vicarage doorbell. Jordan invited her in and enquired whether she would like a cup of tea or coffee.

'Tea please,' she replied, feeling more like she needed a double whisky to get her through this. While he went to make it, she surveyed his study. She had never seen so many books, of all shapes and sizes. She wondered whether he had read them all.

Their discussion covered all sorts of aspects of the Christian life. Jordan thought to himself, this is a tough one, but also thought it would be nice to have a female baptised, as it was nearly always blokes lately. Even the normally hostile *Tamworth Gazette* was interested in making some sort of story of it all.

Jordan did not want to be pushy, but he did want some sort of decision from Freya. In the end it came down to a matter of faith. Did Freya have a real faith in Christ? He was doubtful, but he concluded he had to have faith in the person being baptised.

Together they read through *So You Were Not Done as a Child?* and read some Bible verses. Suddenly Freya said, 'OK, I'll do it!'

So a date was set for 10.30am on the Sunday in three weeks' time. 'I'll let you know if I change my mind,' was her parting shot, hoping in some ways that she could get out of it.

As she was leaving, Craven arrived, looking as athletic as ever in a blue tracksuit. Freya greeted him warmly and told him she had agreed to being baptised and the date had been fixed.

'Praise the Lord,' muttered Craven under his breath.

'What was that?' exclaimed Freya.

'Oh nothing. I'm delighted. We must have a party to celebrate!' They agreed he could call at her flat later that evening.

When she got home and had sorted through the day's junk mail, she noticed there was a letter with a German postmark. It must be from Uncle Franz in Leipzig, thought Freya. He was her mother's younger brother who rarely wrote and whom she saw even less. Franz explained that he had only just got round to sorting out some of her mother's things, which Freya had not dealt with three years ago. Among them was her mother's

Bible. In it, he explained, he had found the enclosed. Freya tore open the inner envelope, and inside was a stiff piece of paper headed 'St George's church, Leipzig', and on which was written in German, 'Certificate of Baptism' and the following text:

> This is to certify that on 21st October 1977 Freya Elisabeth Angella Bloomstatte was baptised according to the rights of the Lutheran Church of Germany. Signed Helmut Gronberg.

There were details of godparents and some other information. Freya felt in a state of shock. What should she do? Forget it, or go ahead with her baptism? She desperately wanted to share her dilemma.

A ring on the doorbell interrupted her musings. She opened it, and in strode Mac!

The red-top newspaper

Frank, who loathed shopping, was encouraged by Liz to wait outside the mini-market while she popped in 'for a few things'. Frank, who had been happy to take early retirement from the electrical firm on a reasonable pension after 35 years in personnel, duly sat on the vacant seat. Some of the town's litter swirled around the windy arcade. He didn't know whether to be public spirited enough to pick some of it up and put it in a waste bin if he could see one nearby.

Eventually he decided it was someone else's job; after all, these council workers were paid enough. He paid his council taxes for them to work, and they often seemed to be threatening to go on strike!

His eye was caught by a sheet or two of a newspaper which had become stuck under his seat. 'Councillor in sex scandal,' it proclaimed in bold black letters. Normally he would avert his eyes from such material, but he saw the name of Nick Dobson and a photo of a topless female. Frank picked the paper up and read it avidly, telling himself he was interested in the character of Nick Dobson and not in the picture of some buxom female.

Nick Dobson had been in the same class as Frank at school. He had always been an ambitious character, heading up the debating society even at the age of 16. He progressed through the lower echelons of his political party, was elected County Councillor some ten years ago and became leader after only two years.

Fancy Nick getting into trouble like that – I wonder who the girl is? he thought. Frank read on and discovered that her name was Cherry Bule, aged 23, from a town not far away.

Just at that point Liz emerged, carrying far more shopping

than she had expected to purchase. 'Frank,' she murmured, but could not see him. All she could see was someone sitting on the nearby seat reading a newspaper – one of those filthy, filthy, tabloids, she thought. She wondered why the government allowed such things to be printed. Just at that moment, Frank heard his name. What to do now – stay behind the paper, or face Liz and her anger?

He decided with some hesitation to do the former and saw Liz disappear round the corner and briefly out of sight. What to do with the paper? He didn't want to be seen carrying it to a bin so, in his haste, he screwed it up and put it in his overcoat pocket. Liz spotted him and cried, 'Where have you been?'

'Just around the corner, dear,' was all he could muster by way of reply.

'Gazing into those women's underwear shops, no doubt!' she snapped. Frank was silent but offered his hand to carry the shopping back to the car.

The history of Frank and Liz's relationship was an interesting one. They had met at a singles' holiday week. Neither had been in a serious relationship before, but on a ramble with others they had got into friendly conversation and had sat on the same table for the rest of the week. At the time, Liz was working for an American-based organisation called CHI, which stood for Children's Health International. Frank was impressed, especially when she said she had recently been on a trip to Jordan with the director.

'And what do you do?' she enquired, more out of politeness than interest.

'Oh, I just work in the personnel department of a firm. Nothing much really; been there since I left school. It's a job. Not as important as yours sounds.'

Liz let it pass that she was not actually number two to the director of the organisation. The policy had always been to allow the director to take one member of staff, preferably female, on an annual fact-finding trip abroad. Expenses and overheads always seemed to consume a large part of the income of the organisation, but these were often masked in the accounts when they were published.

Liz gloated in the minor fame she seemed to have achieved in Frank's eyes. As the week went on they felt more and more comfortable in each other's company. There was, in fact, no physical contact whatsoever until the last morning, when they shook hands, and Frank dared to ask whether they could meet up again. 'We only live 20 miles apart. We could have lunch and a walk together.'

'Yes, that would be nice,' Liz replied, quite enthusiastically.

'What about the Dragon Arms, just outside Chippenham on the A568?' asked Frank.

'Sorry, I don't do pubs,' Liz responded, nearly adding that she thought they were horrible places, but just stopping herself.

'Come to my place, then, and I'll cook us a meal.'

The courtship progressed without any real physical contact. After a year, Frank plucked up courage to ask Liz if he could marry her. She hesitated for quite a while and then said, 'I'll have to go home and pray about it.'

'Pray about it!' exclaimed Frank.

Praying and Frank did not fit very well together. He had given up on religion at around the age of ten when his mother died. If there was a god out there somewhere, why didn't he save his mum? He surely could not exist, Frank concluded. And that had been his philosophy for the last 30 or so years. 'OK,' he said in a somewhat taut voice. 'Goodbye,' and attempted to kiss her, which she stubbornly refused.

A week later, Liz emailed him. 'The answer is yes!' was all it said. Frank was pleased but at the same time saddened by the way it was conveyed. What should have been a special moment was rather flattened by her matter-of-fact approach. However, they did meet up for a quiet meal after going to buy an engagement ring.

Frank's sister Daphne heard the news with great excitement. 'We must have a party!' she screamed. 'I'll organise it!'

Until now, Liz had not met any of Frank's family, except a brief visit to his father in a local nursing home. The news of the impending 'party' filled her with horror, but she had not reckoned with Daphne and her organising skills.

The party took place in the local social club, with lots of Daphne's friends plus a couple of Frank's ex-workmates. Nobody had thought of inviting any of Liz's family – if, indeed, she had any. When the happy couple arrived, the party was in full swing. There were balloons everywhere, bunting and banners and tables groaning with food, and there was drink in abundance. The disco was so loud nobody could make themselves heard. Eventually Jason, Daphne's 21-year-old son, quietened everyone down and proposed a toast. 'To Frank and Liz and their future happiness.'

Frank looked around him and pondered, so if this is what an engagement party is like, what on earth is married life going to be like, and especially the wedding day?

He found a few words to say which, in a way, surprised him. He thanked people for coming – especially Daphne, who revelled in the adulation. In the meantime, Liz looked on somewhat bemused, managing a faint smile from time to time. Smiling was not usually on her agenda, but she made a brave effort on this occasion.

'Go on, Frank, give her a big kiss,' yelled Karl, Daphne's rather loud-mouthed son-in-law. 'Good practice for the wedding night, but you've probably been at it for weeks, mate.'

It was difficult to say who was the more embarrassed. Liz submitted to a light kiss on the cheek, but even that was with some trepidation.

'Go on, you can snog better than that!' Karl was in full flight, ably supported by his cronies from the rugby club. 'Want me to show you how it's done?'

That was enough for Frank and Liz and they both rushed from the building into the cool autumn air. Once outside, Frank did give Liz a 'proper kiss', as he called it.

'Now that's enough,' said Liz.

As they got to the car park the sound of the disco was still blaring. 'Someone seems to be having a good time, but I don't think it's us,' was Frank's final comment.

The wedding took place in early spring and, after the experience of the engagement party, they were careful who they invited. Daphne was invited but declined as she had felt rather unwell lately. Karl was on tour with his rugby club so there were no more than 15 guests. The service in a local Methodist church was well conducted and the reception in the church hall had been organised by Liz, whose taste was very different to that of Daphne – no alcohol and strictly vegetarian.

'If this is what you want, who am I to interfere?' was Frank's comment when Liz shared her plans with him.

The honeymoon was only three days, as Liz considered that any longer would be extravagant. A short stay at Mrs Marshall's B & B establishment in Marefield Bay was all she required.

On the last night of their so-called honeymoon they did, in fact, consummate their marriage. Previously Liz had cried, 'Don't come near me!' Nevertheless, she would not be seen unclothed, and it was over very quickly. Messy, thought Liz. It was, in fact, the only time in their marriage, and neither mentioned it in future years. Indeed, Liz had insisted on single beds from the start, and always managed to get into her bed before Frank came into the room, and locked the door when she was taking a bath or a shower.

To many they appeared to be a happy couple – at least, that was the impression given to neighbours and friends. Even Daphne thought they looked happy, yet, underneath, there was deep unease. There was a lack of trust which reached into every part of their lives. At the outset Liz had demanded control of the finances. True, they now had a joint bank account, which had been negotiated with some difficulty and not without some tears. At their wedding service the preacher had emphasised that 'two shall become one', but in reality it was very different. Very little was shared and it was a long way from what it could be. It was not exactly a brother–sister relationship, but it was a lot less than family and neighbours assumed it to be.

'What on earth is this doing in your pocket?' Liz held up the screwed-up piece of newspaper Frank had hurriedly stuffed into his coat when she had arrived in the shopping mall.

'I... I... er, I...' he stammered. 'I just picked it up because it was littering the area, and I couldn't see a bin.'

'I don't believe you!' exploded Liz. (Believing Frank was not something Liz did very easily.)

Frank attempted to explain that, in reality, he had picked it up because he saw his old school pal, Nick Dobson's name on it.

'That's as may be.' But Liz was doubly outraged when she realised it was Frank who had been hiding behind the newspaper when she was looking for him. 'That does it!' she exclaimed loudly, slamming the lounge door behind her.

It was now Frank's turn to be near to tears. Yes, his eyes had taken more than a cursory glance at the beautiful woman in the Nick Dobson story. Yes, he had concealed himself from Liz; yes, he did know that marriage could be better than this; yes, since retirement life had been empty; yes, they did belong to various organisations like U3A and a music club, and Liz had her church where she seemed to be so often, and not just on

Sundays. However, deep down, life was rather empty, dull and a bit boring. What should he do? Who could he turn to? He had prayed once or twice in his life, but he did not seem to get any answers.

Just then he had what he later described as 'a brill thought'. Why not ring Nick Dobson and say how sorry he was for the mess he had got himself into. Being a local councillor it was easy to find his number. Nick Dobson's answerphone simply said, 'Councillor Dobson is not available at present, but if you leave your name and number, he will return your call as soon as possible.'

Frank felt let down and picked up a book he had borrowed from the local library – *Understanding Made Easy* by Dr Hubert Carter PHD DSC IFRAS. Frank surveyed the contents and started to read the preface: 'We all want to understand the world we live in – politics, the environment, trade, history, economics, even ourselves,' it began. 'I can tell you everything you need to know about understanding itself.'

Must be American, thought Frank, not realising the author was British. Nevertheless he read on. The author wrote from a seemingly 'know-it-all' position, but Frank drank in every word.

'Consider your life,' it said, 'your dreams, hopes and values. Are they what they should be?'

No, thought Frank. He paused for a moment to consider the reason he was dissatisfied in life. His home, his retirement, his marriage, his community and his hopes – they were all something less than they could be.

'In my opinion,' the author continued, and Frank realised the celebrated Dr Carter had plenty of those! 'In my opinion, there are thousands, maybe millions, of people whose expectations have yet to be fulfilled. Reader, you could be one of those.' Here Frank thought he was indeed speaking to him. 'I would advise...' There was much use of the personal pronoun.

He does seem to be over-confident about his opinions, he does seem knowledgeable about all sorts of things, and he could even be talking about me, thought Frank.

Just then the phone rang. 'Nick Dobson here, Frank, just returning your call.'

'How nice to hear from you,' replied Frank. Suddenly they were into conversation as though it were only yesterday, catching up on the news of what must have been decades. At no point was the scandal that had made the front page of at least one tabloid newspaper even mentioned.

'Look here, Frank, why don't we have lunch together? What about tomorrow?'

Frank was just about to reply that Liz would not approve, when he heard himself say, 'OK.'

'What about the Greyhound, say 12.30pm?'

In no time it was agreed, and Frank began to wonder how he should tell Liz, a prospect he did not really relish. When he did at last pluck up the courage to tell her, she replied with all the haughtiness she could muster. 'Nick Dobson? Nick Dobson! His name is plastered all over the papers – all those sex scandals.' She put it in the plural for added effect. Frank was just about to reply it was only one newspaper, and that it was one that appealed to the lower end of the market, when Liz continued, 'Well, if you *must* see him, don't be out all the afternoon.'

The rest of the day passed with a weary monotony, Frank watching football on TV, Liz glued to her book.

Frank could not wait for the next day, and he was at the Greyhound in good time. If Nick was involved in such a scandal why had the local newspapers and the local radio not reported it? Was there any truth in the tabloid account? He had secretly salvaged the offensive paper from the recycling bin (Liz was ultra-keen on recycling) and had studied it again. Yes, it looked like the Nick he had known at school, and as far as he could remember he had heard he was a happily married family man.

At that moment, Nick arrived, smartly dressed in a casual manner, and greeted Frank warmly. 'How are you, old chap? I won't say you don't look any older than when we last met – what was it, 25 years ago?' Nick was all smiles and his greeting seemed really genuine. 'How is Elizabeth? My wife knew her when she worked at the local chemist many years ago – "Betty Boots" she was nicknamed. I hope I'm not treading on corns, but she seemed very prim and proper in those days, but I expect your marriage has relaxed her just a little.'

Wish it had, thought Frank. 'She's fine,' he replied, without much enthusiasm.

'Now what will you have? We'll share the lunch bill, but drinks are on me,' replied Nick.

Settled in a corner they surveyed the menu which was extensive, but not overpriced. 'Steak and ale pie,' said Frank after not much thought.

'Make that two,' said Nick as the waitress took their order.

Frank took a long, long sip of his pint of best bitter, something that had been denied him much of his married life. Nick was directing the conversation. 'I ought to come clean,' he confided, in a voice loud enough for Frank to hear but out of earshot of other customers. You'll have seen the splash on the front page of the tabloid. I can tell you I was very, very, hurt by it, but perhaps you'd care to look at this.' Nick produced a cutting from the same paper. It read:

> We wish to apologise to Mr Nick Dobson for the article featuring him. It was meant to read Mr Mick Dobson, his twin brother, who is not and never has been a county councillor. Councillor Nick Dobson has been offered a full apology and has generously donated the £5,000 offered in compensation to

charity. This apology is also extended to his aged parents, his wife and family.

'Sadly, the apology was not printed on the front page! But never mind,' said Nick. 'Now drink up and tell me your news.'

'Not much to tell,' replied Frank. 'Liz and I have been married 11 years now. We jog along OK. Now we're retired we do all the retiree things like U3A. Liz goes to church and seems to spend a lot of time there.'

Conversation slowed as the waitress brought them their meals – huge platefuls which they tucked into with great relish.

Eventually Frank enquired about Nick's life and his family and commented how different he seemed to be to his sibling. Nick replied that he and his brother were always being confused – even at his wedding when Mick had been his best man. A female guest had confused him with the bridegroom, a remark that Mick had overheard and enjoyed, since he and marriage did not go too well together. He'd had a series of short-term relationships, but only one divorce he could remember. 'I'm afraid I spend a lot of time getting Mick out of trouble, but this time it's gone a bit too far.'

'Don't say that,' said Frank, but without conviction, thinking of his own loveless marriage and Mick's string of unhappy alliances and, as far as he could see, Nick's matrimonial bliss. What an odd triangle, he thought. Surely everyone has the right to be happy. Or do they? Are some people, like me, predestined to go through life as perpetual losers?

Frank returned to earth, as it were, when the waitress brought the dessert menu. 'I'm very tempted by the banoffee pie with whisky sauce,' mused Frank.

'Why not?!' exclaimed Nick. 'Two please, and coffee.'

Conversation slowed somewhat after lunch and Frank was loath to enquire too much into Nick's council work or anything else, except that he was rather curious. He wanted to know what made this guy tick.

After the meal they returned to a quiet corner of the bar for their coffee when Nick said he was a councillor for two reasons. 'First of all I was elected, and secondly, I feel I want to serve the community.'

'I can agree with the first, but aren't all politicians out for their own ends?' said Frank, who had developed a cynical view about life in general, and those in any kind of authority in particular.

'Have you been drinking, Frank?' was the greeting from Liz when Frank returned home. Liz had a horror of alcohol which manifested itself from time to time.

'Look, Liz,' Frank attempted to explain. 'I met up for lunch with Nick Dobson, and we had a pint or two by way of remembering old times.'

'Huh,' was all Liz could mutter.

'That's not much of a greeting when I come home,' was Frank's retort, and they each departed to separate parts of the house – he to the garage and to various DIY tasks that had been waiting for ages to be completed; she to the lounge to continue reading her book, *Into a Real Relationship* by Rev Dr Simon Portas. Whatever the book taught or advised, Liz tried to ignore, especially the chapter on 'meaningful forgiveness'. Whatever does he know about real life, she almost spat out.

'Hello, darling, can I help you with your shopping?' the words came from a middle-aged man, about Frank's age. Liz wanted to say no immediately, but held back a second or two before saying, 'Er, er, no thank you, no.'

'Well, you look very laden. Won't you let me help?'

'Well, alright, just as far as the bus station.' She was very suspicious of most strangers, especially men, but there was actually something rather attractive about this one. Very few people offered to help these days, she thought, and Frank often let her struggle unnecessarily.

'I'm Mick, by the way.'

'Liz,' was her one-word reply, as she shook hands in such a way as to ensure as little contact as possible.

'Let's go for a coffee,' said Mick, and before Liz realised what was happening she was sitting sipping a cappuccino.

Well, she thought, a man – a complete stranger, to boot – offering to carry my bags and treating me to a coffee. That hasn't happened for a long, long time, not since the days of Frank's and my courtship, if that's what you could call it.

Liz looked round the room, hoping no one would recognise her, but in the corner she spied Celia who lived just across the road. Liz gave her a half-hearted wave, secretly hoping the ground would open up and swallow her, for Celia was, in fact, the biggest gossip in her neighbourhood. Celia could not wait to get out of the coffee shop to enlighten her circle on the fact that an ever-so-upright person such as Liz was hobnobbing with another man. Liz called her over. 'Celia, this is my cousin Mick,' but the words were lost as Celia swept out with all thoughts of further purchases abandoned for the day.

'What's this about being your cousin?' said Mick.

'Oh, nothing really, only our neighbour is a terrible gossip and the next thing will be that Frank will hear I've kept another man company.'

'Very pleasant company, if I may say so,' replied Mick. 'Another cup?'

'Well, perhaps just a small one,' replied Liz weakly.

This handsome man was paying attention to her in a way few others had done. The conversation just flowed, until suddenly Liz cried, 'Heavens, is that the time? I must get back to get Frank's lunch.'

'Can't he get it himself?' was Mick's response. 'Here, use my mobile and tell him you've met an old friend.'

'I can't do that, and besides, you're not an old friend.'

'Well, you can tell him you've made a new friend.'

Before she could respond she found herself dialling her home number and leaving a hesitant recorded message to the effect that she wouldn't be home for a while and could he get his own lunch just this once.

'Look, my car is in the multi. I'll get it and you can put your shopping in the boot, and we can drive out into the country and get some lunch.'

Liz opened her mouth to say no, but actually responded with a weak 'OK.'

Mick's car was a make Liz did not recognise but it was modern, sleek and very comfortable. They soon arrived at the pub where Nick and Frank had dined a few days ago. After they had parked, Mick held open the car door and helped Liz out.

How attentive, thought Liz.

What nice legs, thought Mick.

Before long they were studying the menu in a quiet corner of the bar. 'What would you like to drink?' enquired Mick.

'Oh, just a fruit juice please,' Liz replied. 'I don't really drink alcohol,' she added, somewhat moderating her stance from her reproachful attack on Frank a few days previously.

'Fruit juice for me because I'm driving, but you must have a large glass of red wine. They have a fairly decent cellar here, so my brother tells me.'

'Oh alright, just one.' Liz felt herself being drawn into a situation where she was losing control, at least just a bit. Good job Frank can't see me now, she thought.

The wine had quite gone to her head by the time they settled over coffee. 'Tell me about your brother. Is he as charming as you?' Realising what she had said, she was relieved when Mick reluctantly ignored the compliment.

'Well, we're identical twins and often get mistaken for each other. He's a county councillor and has achieved a lot; he's very different from me. I won't go into my past, but in many ways we're as different as chalk and cheese.'

Liz wanted him to go on but was conscious of the time, and she knew Frank would begin to wonder where she was. Courteous as ever, Mick helped her into the car. 'Liz,' he said gently, and drew her into his arms. She felt a guilty thrill as he kissed her passionately, but at last she pushed him away.

'Take me home please,' she said, and he duly obeyed.

'See you again soon.' She half nodded but knew it was not to be, as she walked the 100 yards from the bus stop to her home.

Frank was in the workshop and she popped her head around the door. 'Have you been drinking? Who have you been with? Don't deny it.' Frank was angry as well as curious, since Celia had called an hour earlier and divulged that she had seen Mick and Liz in the coffee shop. Celia did not really need a pretext to call, but made the excuse of needing to borrow a mousetrap. 'Your hair's in a mess and your lipstick is smudged. What have you been up to?'

There was no reply as Liz rushed indoors and bolted the bathroom door behind her.

An hour or so later (it seemed much longer to Frank) she emerged looking rather crestfallen. The rest of the day passed in a sort of armed truce with as few words spoken as possible.

The next day was Sunday and Liz began to get ready for church as usual. They had both had a sleepless night and the domestic atmosphere was little better than the previous day.

'Mind if I come with you?' said Frank, out of the blue.

'Why, er, yes, if you wish,' said Liz, completely taken aback. Going to church was something Frank never did unless he had to. He had gone reluctantly to the wedding of Liz's niece and would go to the occasional funeral if he could not find an excuse to get out of it, but going on a Sunday was definitely not for him. He kept asking himself why Liz had behaved so strangely the day before. From his viewpoint Christians did not behave like that. Although the atmosphere was somewhat less frosty, there was a frigidity which endured.

They arrived after the service had started, and Frank insisted that they sit in the back row and at the end.

Liz was more than a little alarmed that the smartly dressed man sitting at the front looked so like the man with whom she had spent some illicit moments the day before. Could it be? No, it can't be. She was almost ready to run out of the church but was afraid of the commotion it would cause, so she smiled weakly at her friend Sheila in the next pew.

Frank mouthed the hymns, mumbled the Amen at the end of the prayers, studied the stained glass during the readings and avoided any sort of eye contact with anyone else.

The pastor then announced that they were continuing their study on human relationships and today they were thinking about 'forgiveness', and he was delighted to welcome Mr Nick Dobson, who was their local county councillor. Liz let out a brief sigh as she realised that this was not the man she had been with so recently. She and Frank even managed half a smile at each other. Was the ice breaking? Frank did not seem to know; nor did Liz.

Nick's sermon was simple and straight to the point. He ended with a plea and a prayer that anyone who needed to forgive or to be forgiven by God or others could have that experience in the silence that followed. An incredible hush descended on the congregation, broken only by the sound of two people sobbing their hearts out in the back row.

Battle of the exes

Cartwright, senior partner of Cartwright, Solomon & Cartwright, always opened his office early on New Year's Day. His secretary, Denise, came in even earlier to answer the phone and make sure Mr Cartwright had everything to hand when the first clients arrived at 9.30am – which they always did. For many years his firm had advertised its services in the local media at Christmas, knowing there was a ready market over the festive season. The day before, Denise had popped in to make a list of appointments so that everything was ready on his desk. Denise herself did not mind working on public holidays. She lived alone with her two cats and three dogs, and she appreciated being paid triple time for her trouble.

The first couple, Sandy and Michaela, appeared from different directions and avoided all eye contact with each other. Seated uncomfortably in the office of Mr Cartwright, Michaela blurted out, 'I want a divorce!'

'Well, I don't,' replied Sandy, before Mr Cartwright could get a word in.

Eventually, after a pause in the ensuing heated discussion, he did enquire about the reasons. Why, he asked, did they, especially Michaela, want the marriage terminated?

Mich, as she liked to be known, uttered just two words: 'unreasonable behaviour'. She shouted them so loudly that Denise, in the next room, could hear quite clearly. Denise had worked for so many years for the firm that she was never surprised at the behaviour of various couples, and she privately thanked God (in whom she really did not believe) that she was unwed. They came, they argued (sometimes over the most superficial things, like a dog's bed), they cried, they stormed out. And so it went on day after day. What did they promise on their wedding day? she thought. Did they even know what they had promised?

Just then there was a knock at the side door. It was Debbie, the cleaner. Denise opened it, somewhat surprised to see her. 'Sorry I'm late,' said a flustered Debbie, 'but it's school hols and I had to get someone to look after Ryan. I didn't know you worked on New Year's Day!'

'We don't usually, but Mr Cartwright has a lot of clients who need to see him urgently.'

Debbie was just about to ask why when she realised that at New Year a lot of marriages split up and people need legal advice.

Debbie was 25 and a very attractive brunette who had taken the cleaning job after Andy had walked out six months earlier. Ryan, their son, was a lively six-year-old who obviously missed his father, but was adored by Debbie's parents who lived too far away to provide any practical day-to-day help. Debbie felt very vulnerable and alone and without any real friends. The company she enjoyed at bingo did not provide real friendship, and anyway that had to end when her income from Andy suddenly decreased. They had never married, mainly because they had agreed that so many of the married couples they knew seemed to be unhappy or were going through the process of divorce.

Then she had noticed a poster advertising 'Kidscope' – an after-school club for five- to eight-year-olds. Just the thing for Ryan, she thought, if she could get a job for, say, two hours a day. That was the second amazing thing to happen, when she responded to an advert for a job at the offices of Cartwright, Solomon & Cartwright. It was Mr Cartwright Junior who had interviewed her, stressing the importance of security and confidentiality, as she would be working in offices which had sensitive material lying about on desks. Somehow Debbie managed to track down a former teacher at her secondary school and a neighbour who gave her the necessary references, and she started work two months after Andy left.

Andy had jobs that took him to building sites across the country. He occasionally sent money for Ryan's upkeep, and even less frequently came to visit. Visits, when they did occur, were never lacking in tension. Debbie had a fatalistic streak in her nature, perhaps inherited from her parents. That's my lot in life, she thought. Que sera sera.

The people at Kidscope were bright, interested and warm-hearted. Before long Debbie began to make friends, although very cautiously at first, because she did not want anyone to know her recent history. She began to notice that one or two of the leaders seemed to have a calm and gentle authority, which she could not really place.

Kidscope took place every afternoon and was obviously a fun time for the 20 or 30 children who came, some of whose parents appeared to have situations similar to her own. Debbie had only been vaguely aware that Kidscope was a play on words – that children can 'cope'. It took place in a church hall which had recently been extensively refurbished. It was clean and welcoming and not at all like some church buildings, thought Debbie.

After two or three weeks, Debbie got into conversation with Fran, one of the leaders, who was in her late forties with grown-up children. She was a fully rounded woman in more ways than one. Fran explained that Kidscope had been going for several years and was part of the outreach of St Agatha's, the Anglican church next door. What on earth does she mean by 'outreach'? thought Debbie.

Back home she got out an old dictionary and looked up 'outreach'. It said 'propagating take-up of a service by seeking out appropriate people and persuading them to accept what is judged good for them.'

Debbie read it through several times and concluded she was little wiser – words like 'propagating' and 'appropriate' would need further investigation, and she rapidly became uninterested and put the book away. It wasn't that she disliked words as such – she even attempted the crossword in her women's magazine from time to time – but she felt that people who went to the church used a certain type of language which she did not understand – or, if she was truly honest, did not want to understand.

So each day, Debbie took Ryan to Kidscope, meeting him at the school gates and then afterwards taking him to a neighbour while she cleaned at Cartwright, Solomon & Cartwright. The firm were good to her and after a month Mr Cartwright stayed on to meet her and to inform her that a) the job was permanent and b) they were very pleased with her work.

So life settled down to something of a routine, and only the weekends were something of a trial. Debbie never knew if Andy would ring or call, so she was kept on tenterhooks until Monday. Ryan enjoyed walks in the park and watching football, which Debbie loathed, but the weather was often a deterrent. One sunny Sunday morning they did happen to pass St Agatha's, and Ryan asked if they were going to Kidscope. Debbie explained that Kidscope only operated as an after-school club and today was Sunday. 'Well, let's go in the church then,' he said.

'No, we can't do that. They wouldn't want us there. It's really only for old women,' Debbie replied, forgetting, of course, that the people who ran Kidscope weren't old at all, especially her new friend Fran, who was in her forties.

'But,' persisted Ryan, 'I can see children like me in there, and teenagers.' (He was not quite sure what teenagers were, but he assumed they were children who were not yet quite grown up.) 'Look, there's Fran.' As they looked across the road from the park, it seemed St Agatha's had a certain magnetic attraction.

'Come on,' said Debbie, 'we'll miss the start of the game. It's the Wheatsheaf team playing and they're top of the league.' So they went off to watch football.

'Mum,' enquired Ryan that afternoon, 'why didn't we go into the church?'

'Didn't I tell you it's for old people?' she replied.

'Fran doesn't look that old!' Ryan was indeed a persistent lad.

'Look, Ryan, perhaps I was mistaken. Perhaps it's not for old people, but it is for posh ones; not for the likes of you and me.'

This seemed to quieten Ryan for a bit, but after a while he came back with, 'But Fran isn't a bit posh, and anyway, I saw some of my friends from Kidscope there.'

'Alright then, Ryan.' Debbie felt her irritation rising. 'We'll go one day.'

This seemed to pacify Ryan until bedtime when he asked, 'Can we go next Sunday? We can miss football just this once.'

'I'm not making any promises. Goodnight, Ryan.' And, after the briefest of kisses, she went out and closed the door.

The next day, as she dusted and vacuumed round Mr Cartwright Senior's office, she found a sheet of paper which had slipped underneath the desk. Not wanting to leave it there she picked it up and was just about to put it in the recycling bin when she noticed the words 'Strictly Confidential' at the top and a date only four days old. Curiosity got the better of her and she read on. *In the Case of Frances Jane Speedwell and Jermaine Speedwell -v- Frederick Samuel Light.* Debbie blinked, she could not believe her eyes.

Frances Jane was the Fran of Kidscope and Frederick Samuel was Andy's father! She read on, but the 'heretofore' and 'in consideration of' and other legal wording baffled her. What should she do? She knew there was a photocopier next door, but was uncertain how to work it. She did not know what it was about, or how Fran and Freddy, as he liked to be called, had got involved with each other.

She had seen Freddy in the street a couple of times since Andy had left but, apart from a brief 'Hi,' from her and a grunt from him, that was all the acknowledgment there was of each other. When she was living with Andy, however, Freddy seemed to spend lots of time with them. He made a point of seeing Ryan at least twice a week and was always there for Sunday lunch. Yet Freddy never seemed to reciprocate the hospitality. He was a widower in his sixties, had been unemployed for four to five years and had got into a mindset that work and he did not really agree. The lady at the Job Centre was always encouraging him and offered all sorts of opportunities either to retrain or simply to get on the employment ladder, but while he could get several meals a week at Debbie and Andy's home, he did not bother. He did have other options with Andy's sister, but she limited his visits to once a month. His other indulgence was a beer and chips once a week at his working men's club, or non-working men's club as he called it. Once Andy had walked away, visits fizzled out and Freddy now saw very little of Ryan and Debbie.

All this recent history flashed through Debbie's mind. What should she do? Put the paper back where she had found it? That would indicate she had never cleaned round there. Take it? Destroy it? These were options she quickly dismissed. In the end she turned it face down and put it under one of the legal books on Mr Cartwright's desk with the corner showing so that Mr Cartwright would find it when he came in next morning and would assume he had put it there in the first place.

On the way home Debbie wondered what the dispute could be. On the one hand Fran was at least 15 years younger than Freddy. She was kind and friendly and very much committed to community service. By contrast, there was Freddy, who

Debbie, perhaps unfairly, labelled a scrounger. She felt that she did not want to get involved with Andy's dad again, partly because she had noticed a difference in her finances, both negatively and positively, since Andy had left. Negatively in that Andy only paid for Ryan's upkeep, but positively that she was only feeding two instead of three – often four when Freddy came around. With the money from her cleaning job she just about made ends meet, though it was quite tight sometimes.

The paper she had found in Mr Cartwright's office really got to her, and affected her sleep patterns. Even Ryan noticed a difference. 'What's wrong, Mum?' he would ask before he went to sleep. 'Do you miss Dad?'

Debbie replied, 'Yes, I do.'

Ryan blurted out, 'So do I,' and, after a pause, 'very much.' Tears came to both their eyes and they gave each other a big hug before Ryan closed his eyes and eventually drifted off to sleep.

Debbie thought for a moment and asked herself, Do I really miss him? and concluded, Yes, I do, but not Andy's dad! Sleep eluded her until the early hours.

The next time she took Ryan to Kidscope, Debbie tried to avoid Fran as much as she was able. There seemed to be more and more mums and occasionally one or two dads coming along. There was time given for children to talk about their problems, if they wanted, to Maggie, a grandmotherly sort in her late sixties who made herself available but was unobtrusive. She just listened as was needed.

Debbie managed to retreat into the kitchen to make drinks and cupcakes with a few of the older children. But as much as she tried to escape she knew that, before long, she would have to face Fran. How? and When? continued to be the dominant questions in her mind. And what do you do when you know something of someone's secret? Curiosity demands that you want to know more, but reluctance to interfere prevents anything being said.

After a week or so, Fran asked, 'Debbie – what's wrong?' Fran was all concern. 'You seem to be avoiding me. Is it anything I've said or done?' Debbie was indeed aware that an invisible wall had arisen between them, a barrier that Fran did not know about. 'Is it about Ryan? He seems to be getting along so well here at Kidscope. Is it school? Do you want to tell me?'

This was too much for Debbie, who burst into tears and fled to the loo. Incidents like this were not uncommon at Kidscope, mainly with the parents and sometimes with the children. Fran waited a minute for Debbie to reappear and then went to talk to Maggie who, although she had seen it happen many times before, still felt more than a degree of heartache, since nearly all at Kidscope came from broken families.

Debbie, meanwhile, emerged and realised it was time to pack up and take Ryan home in time for her cleaning shift. 'What's up, Mum?' Ryan, although only six, was a sensitive lad in terms of both his own family and the hurts of others.

'Oh, it's nothing, Ryan,' but he knew somehow that was not true.

Debbie left Ryan with her neighbour, Sonia, and arrived at the office. She was amazed to see Mr Cartwright Senior's car still in the car park. Not like him to work late, she thought, as she tapped in the pass code to let herself in. She went to the cleaning cupboard and had hardly turned the key in the lock when Mr Cartwright appeared at her shoulder. 'Debbie, would you come into my office please?' Debbie could not discern his expression – was it anger or pleasure? Whatever it was, she knew that it was important. These days Mr Cartwright did not work the hours he used to and it must be something special to keep him here so late.

'Please sit down, Debbie.' Debbie had dusted and cleaned the seating in the plush office many times, but had never dared to try to sit down! Other people in such mundane jobs had told her how they had tried out the seating, often 'play acting' the role of the boss, giving imaginary staff instructions, such as to a hidden secretary: 'Bring in my coffee please, Miss Jones.' One of her acquaintances, Angie, had even been caught on camera, and paid the consequences.

'Debbie, I just want to thank you for finding the document and putting it somewhere safe for me.' Debbie was just about to say, 'It was nothing,' but Mr Cartwright continued. 'Here is a little token for your honesty and diligence,' he said, handing her an envelope with the firm's logo on the front. Debbie was a little uncertain what 'diligence' meant, but it sounded OK. Mr Cartwright was in full flight. 'Now you can forget your cleaning this evening. You can catch up another time. I've told my secretary she can empty the waste bins tomorrow. Go home and spend time with your little boy – Ryan, isn't it? We shall see that you get paid for this evening.' With that, he got up and held out his hand to say goodbye. Debbie was almost overcome with both confusion and pride and, grasping the envelope, she said goodnight and went on her way home.

Debbie collected Ryan, who was both delighted and surprised to see his mother so soon, and she explained to Sonia that a) she had not got the sack and b) she had simply been given the time off. Then she spent the early evening playing with Ryan and his favourite toys. Ryan felt that something was different with his mum, but at his age he couldn't tell what it was. He was just delighted to have her to himself and to see her smile, something she had been lacking for quite a while.

The next day at Kidscope Debbie was in the same ebullient mood, something of which both Fran and Maggie were soon aware. Maggie could contain her curiosity no longer. 'Debbie, you look very bright and cheerful today. What's the secret? Is it another fella?'

Debbie laughed to herself, thinking of Mr Cartwright and being alone with him. 'No, certainly not!' was her unequivocal reply. Then she thought about being alone with Mr Cartwright Junior – now that was a different scenario altogether!

'No, it's just that I had some unexpected good news which I prefer to keep to myself.' Maggie was never one to jump to conclusions, but she hoped it might be that Andy was coming home again.

As Debbie was putting her coat on she put her hand in her pocket. She discovered to her horror that the envelope from Mr Cartwright had gone. She searched in her handbag and in other pockets but couldn't find it anywhere.

'Is this what you're looking for?' Fran was holding the envelope, with the Cartwright logo clearly visible. Fran, who knew Debbie had an office cleaning job somewhere in the town, was clearly puzzled as to why Debbie was in possession of a letter from a firm with whom she and Jermaine had had a lot of business in recent weeks. Perhaps it was settlement papers between her and Andy, but it didn't feel that bulky. Fran, still bemused, said goodnight, and Debbie and Ryan wended their way home.

Back in her flat Debbie ripped open the envelope and found not only a handwritten letter from Mr Cartwright but also £100 in crisp £20 notes. She did not know whether to laugh or cry. All this for simply putting a letter on his desk, she thought to herself, placing the money safely in her handbag. If there is a god (and I'm very doubtful if he is around any more) he is smiling on me, and after a pause she added, and also on Ryan! This was the nearest that Debbie, in all her 25 rough, tough years, had ever got to praying. Enough surmising, she thought. Better get Ryan to Sonia and me to my office cleaning. I expect there's more to do having missed out on my work last night.

Jermaine and Fran looked at each other across the supper table. They were a conventional couple who did not 'do' TV suppers. Fran said, 'Jer, you remember I told you about Debbie at Kidscope?'

'You mean the one whose fella walked out on her?'

Most of them seem to claim that, Fran thought. 'Debbie has a bright lad called Ryan who seems to have adjusted to life without having his dad around. Well,' Fran paused, 'Debbie had an envelope with our solicitors' firm's logo on it. It had actually dropped out of her pocket and I had the pleasure of giving it back to her. She was delighted. Seemed it was an interesting package, but I didn't think it could be settlement papers. Help! Does she know anything about our case with Mr Light? Debbie calls herself Debbie Rowlands but I think Andy was Andy Light, in which case we may be pursuing her so-say father-in-law. What a situation! What do we do?' It was Fran's turn to be confused.

'Fran, darling, Debbie has nothing to do with Mr Light Senior. Has she ever mentioned him?'

'No, I don't, think so,' came the reply.

'Let's ask Debbie and Ryan round on Sunday, and then we can clear the air.'

'That seems a good idea,' said Fran.

It was now Wednesday and Fran was determined to approach Debbie, but somehow her courage failed her, as it did at Thursday's Kidscope. That evening, Jermaine enquired if Fran had yet invited Debbie and Ryan to come on Sunday. Fran confessed she had not had the courage to do so yet.

'But it's Friday tomorrow and you only have then to ask.' Jer was a patient kind of guy but he was anxious to clear the air. 'Let's pray about it before we go to bed.' That is exactly what they did, but it still meant a sleepless night for Fran, who woke up rather cross and irritable in the morning.

Later at Kidscope, Fran was not her usual self, and now it was Debbie's turn to enquire into Fran's well-being. 'Oh it's nothing,' was Fran's dismissive reply.

'People always say that to cover up when something's wrong,' replied Debbie. There was a very awkward pause and Fran looked away and tried to change the subject.

Debbie began to apologise. 'I'm so sorry to upset you.'

Fran could only say, 'It's nothing to do with you,' and then turned to the matter of registering the children and sorting out toys and games, something she did with an extra amount of vigour. Debbie was very aware of the situation which involved Andy's father. She had often wondered what Fran's husband was like, but Fran rarely mentioned him.

Later, as Debbie and Ryan were leaving, Fran said a rather timid goodbye. 'Oh, Debbie, I was wondering – er...' Debbie waited nervously, wondering what was coming next. 'Would you and Ryan like to come to lunch on Sunday? We'll be back from church in good time. Can you come after footie?'

'Well, yes, that would be very nice. I'll look forward to it, and to meeting Jermaine.'

'One o'clock?' was Fran's parting remark. Then, more as a statement than a question as she went out of the door, 'There's nothing that you don't eat, is there?'

At the office, Debbie got on with her cleaning, hoping there were no more strange letters lying around. She realised there was a deeper motive for Fran's offer of hospitality. Both women were aware of the situation, although neither knew all the details, and both were very reluctant to break the uneasy silence over the whole subject.

At lunch on Sunday Jermaine enquired of Ryan, 'Did you enjoy the football?'

'Yes, it was great, the Plough team won 4-0,' was Ryan's

enthusiastic response. Then he continued, 'Mr Speedwell, I saw you going into that church place. I'd like to come sometime, but my mum won't let me.'

'Oh, we'll have to talk to Mum,' replied Jermaine, whose deep resonant voice sounded both kind and strange to Ryan's young ears.

After lunch Fran suggested they went into the garden as it was a lovely day, and they found some toys for Ryan to play with while Jermaine looked for a ball.

'Fran–'

'Debbie–' Both women virtually exploded with what they had to say. They spoke at the same time saying, 'There's something you should know.' Debbie allowed Fran, as the older woman, to set the pace.

Fran explained that Freddy had been making their life intolerable. He would park his car outside their house for what seemed like hours on end and stare into their lounge. He was even there until quite late at night. This went on for weeks until, at last, Fran and Jermaine went to the police. The police sergeant was very sympathetic but said that, unless Freddy was breaking the law, there was nothing they could do about it. He suggested that a solicitor's letter might be a solution.

'Freddy is a strange, strange, man,' responded Debbie. 'Ryan used to ask sometimes, "Where is Granddad?" but hasn't done so lately. To be honest, I'm rather glad he doesn't come any more; he would eat us out of house and home when he did come.' Then she took courage and continued, 'Fran, I, too, have got something to say. I've seen that letter.'

It was Fran's turn to reel in shock. Debbie went on to explain how she had found the letter in the solicitor's office and rather tremulously said, 'It was none of my business, but I couldn't help it, seeing Freddy's name on it. He's someone I'm beginning to really dislike more and more.' (She nearly said 'despise' but was not sure she understood it.)

'Why should he do the things he did?' Fran asked. 'From what you know of Freddy, did he ever express any strong views – about anything?'

'Well, he did say he hated religion, all teenagers are slobs, and things like that. But not all the time,' she added, trying to sound positive in defence of Freddy.

Fran tried to draw the matter to a close by simply stating that the matter was over and that Freddy had been warned about his behaviour and had ceased to pester them. 'Look Debbie, would you like to come to church with us next Sunday? I'm sure you'd enjoy it. There are a lot of people of your age there, and some of Ryan's friends from Kidscope go.'

Debbie thought for a moment and, plucking courage from somewhere she did not know, said, 'OK – we'll come.'

As the week went on she began to regret her decision. Why on earth had she ever agreed? She saw Fran each day at Kidscope. Fran was friendly, kind and helpful, and it was only at the end of Friday that Fran said cheerfully, 'See you both on Sunday, 10.30am.'

'Yes, fine,' replied Debbie with as much enthusiasm as she could muster.

Saturday was an awful day. In the morning, Ryan went round to Sonia's house to play. In the afternoon, to her surprise, Freddy came to take him out. They exchanged frosty greetings and even frostier goodbyes when Ryan returned.

Debbie thought a lot about what she should wear the following day. Should she borrow a hat? A lot of women wore hats to church, or so she thought. Her wardrobe was limited but, after several attempts, she decided on a blouse and skirt.

Saturday night was a sleepless one. She tossed and turned, wondering this, wondering that. In the next room Ryan slept on, blissfully ignorant of his mother's anguish.

After breakfast, they changed and Debbie enquired if Ryan

would miss his football. 'Not today, Mum,' was his distracted reply as he watched the TV.

Postponing the moment until the last possible time, they arrived at St Agatha's only to find it full. The kind man at the door explained that it was Baptism Sunday and hence there were more people than usual. What's Baptism Sunday? thought Debbie. She had never heard of that before, but was too scared to ask.

They found a seat looking down the aisle. The vicar, whom she had seen at Kidscope a few times, said welcome to everyone. Behind him was what looked like a sort of water tank, tastefully draped in blue cloth. Weird, thought Debbie.

The first hymn was announced, the words of which Debbie found rather strange. The vicar said that the children would stay in for the baptism and then go to their groups. Debbie felt a strange feeling which she could not put into words or tell anyone about. The minister explained what baptism was all about, though Debbie guessed that those around her knew anyway.

'I will now ask the candidates to come forward,' said the minister.

The first was a young woman in her teens, then a young man in his 20s. Debbie had great difficulty in seeing and it was only their backs she could make out, but the last candidate seemed somewhat familiar to her. Just at that moment, Ryan leapt up, as only a six-year-old can do, ran down the aisle and shouted in a voice as loud as he could muster, 'DADDY!'

Jeremy the journalist

Jeremy was a journalist, but not a very good one. His ambition had been to work on a national newspaper, but for the last 34 years he had been an ordinary 'hack' on the *Sunford Chronicle*. These were difficult financial times and, eventually, the new editor had called him into her office and explained that the *Chronicle* was struggling and cutbacks would have to be made. Would Jeremy be willing to either be made redundant or just work three days a week and for less pay?

Though schooled in the hard world of cut-and-thrust journalism, the editor was not hard-hearted and realised that Jeremy had given many, many years of loyal service to the paper. She gave him until the end of the month – in fact, a full ten days, to respond.

Jeremy returned to his bachelor flat and thought and thought and thought. The redundancy package would be generous, having worked there for so many years. But what would he do? He was at an age when few people would employ him, and journalism was the only job he knew. On the other hand, if he only worked three days a week, would there be enough to live on?

He rang his sister, Davina, who urged, 'Take the money, Jeremy. Something will come up.' For Davina, something had come up in the shape of Guy, her third husband, who was an accountant with a large company. The house and car told everyone they were doing quite nicely.

Jeremy rang his old friend Bill, who listened to Jeremy's dilemma. 'Oh, stay on for three days a week. It's your life. It's what you're good at.'

In the end, after more thought, Jeremy took Bill's advice and informed the editor of his decision. She responded by saying, 'I'll keep you on the Local Heroes column, plus Heard Around Town, and some footie reporting, but I'm giving Danny, our new, young, reporter, the main news items.' Jeremy wondered why he was being sidelined in favour of the brash new guy when circulation was so low. Maybe he had been brought in to boost sales with more racy reporting.

Jeremy was delighted he could keep his Heard Around Town column, which was really a summary of local gossip and required a couple of visits to local hostelries, with appropriate expenses claims. He wasn't a 'digging the dirt' type of journalist, but he knew what interested many (though not all) of his readers. Banner headline scandals were for the tabloids but, with all his experience, he used more subtle ways of exposure, usually relying more on hints and leaving his readers to guess.

So Jeremy settled down to his diminished role. The question was, what to do with the days he did not work – get another job if one was going? He had few interests, apart from work and Gus, his ginger cat.

Danny, who seemed to get even brasher in his new job, began to despise Jeremy. These old hacks were alright in their day, he thought, but they don't hit the headlines anymore. Danny, of course, did not express his views directly, but the occasional look from his smart new desk towards Jeremy's old one, now tucked into a corner, said it all: 'I'm the new boy on my way up, hopefully to the editor's chair, and you, old man, are on your way down!'

Here was the beginning of a prime example of the age-old conflict between youth and age, between brashness and experience, between the incomer and the resident member. It is writ large in a thousand scenarios. Jeremy was experienced enough to let it ride. He had seen this sort of thing happen many times before.

It was Friday night, time for Jeremy's weekly visit to the Crown in search of gossip, only he would not describe it as such. The Heard Around Town column had been going for more years than he could remember. For many readers it was the first article they turned to, but for a significant number it was the least attractive part of the paper. It was, however, the part of the work that Jeremy enjoyed the most. Of course, the paper changed his name to Craig, but most of his neighbours and the one or two people he called friends knew who wrote it. The new editor tried to change the name to Dave but it didn't work. The style was so recognisable as Jeremy's that readers knew whose it was.

Jeremy took his pint to his usual corner. Sometimes, though not very often, customers would come and keep him company and share their news. Jeremy felt it was a bit like a Roman Catholic confessional, except he did not sit in a box.

His eye strayed to a young couple he had not seen before. The chap looked to be in his mid-twenties, she a bit younger. Jeremy, in an act of seeming friendliness but really out of a mixture of personal interest and professional curiosity, went over to them and introduced himself as, simply, Jeremy.

'Hello, I'm Mark, and this is Rachel,' was the reply.

After the initial pleasantries were exchanged, Jeremy studied the young man. Good-looking, he thought, well built. What about the nasty scar down his left cheek? She was quite pretty without being outstanding: good looks and with a short enough skirt for the regulars at the bar to give more than half a glance. Jeremy wondered why so many girls who wore miniskirts seemed to spend so much time trying to pull them down over their thighs. Still, he never had understood women.

Mark explained that he had just come to the area as he had signed on for the town football team as their new striker. He had been playing for Manfield reserves for most of last season, but had jumped at the chance of first-team football even if it was two leagues below what he was used to. His daytime job was with K2 Double Glazing which, he said, paid quite well. He had no ambitions to be a full-time professional.

Here, thought Jeremy, was a mini-scoop! Yes, the lads doing the sport section would no doubt headline it on the back page with phrases like 'New Striker for Town' and suitable photographs, but here he was in the Crown with the guy himself!

Rachel, in the meantime, said very little, though she kept giving Mark admiring glances, and the ring on her left hand looked new and shiny, so Jeremy guessed they hadn't been married long. Jeremy was intrigued by the scar on Mark's face. How long had he had it? Who, or what, had caused it? But with his long experience as a hack, he held back for a while, as he preferred his 'clients', as he privately called them, to 'spill the beans' themselves.

Mark offered another drink to Jeremy who politely declined. He always made his one pint last the whole evening, much to the landlord's chagrin. The latter, however, consoled himself that sometimes Jeremy's column featured lines like 'heard in the Crown', and he thought the publicity might be good for trade. However, as far as he was aware, no new customers seemed to appear as a result of Jeremy's articles.

Mark and Rachel were glad of the conversation and the friendliness of Jeremy, not realising his occupation or motives. 'I hope you don't mind me asking, but I can't help noticing that scar on your face?' Jeremy was in his most solicitous mode, but he could see the headline, 'Scarred Striker Signs for Town!' Almost everything was seen in terms of the journalistic equivalent of sound bites. It was in his blood, as his father used to say, even though his father had never broken into the journalistic ranks, preferring to remain a printer all his working life.

'No, I don't mind,' said Mark, trying to hide his resentment at this stranger's request, and also trying to hide Rachel's embarrassment. 'It was actually caused by a teenage fight about eight years ago. I got a broken bottle shoved in my face. It caused a lot of bleeding, and I was in hospital for ten days and had to go back for surgery a couple of times. As a youngster I found it very humiliating. Rachel here has been my rock. I only knew her slightly then but she has seen me through. I'm sure the Town folks will accept me.'

Don't know about that, thought Jeremy to himself. However, sensing he was on to something, he pressed on as gently as he could. Straight questioning was something Jeremy found hard to do, but he knew the value of an indirect approach. A few people would confide in him; alternatively, he had developed a skill, over many years, of getting people to tell him what he needed to hear. 'Did they catch the person who did it?'

'Yes, he got three years in a youth custody centre. I don't bear any resentment, though I do have to live with the scars. I only hope any players I have unfairly tackled are also forgiving!'

Jeremy gave a slight smile; it would not be too difficult to find the attacker and discover what had happened to him over the past eight years. Conversation drifted on to the character of the town, shopping, etc, before Mark and Rachel took their leave, still not knowing much about Jeremy or his occupation.

Back in the office Jeremy put his notes in order and began composing his Heard Around Town column. Danny, who had now assumed the role of sub-sub-editor, saw Jeremy's article and thought he could improve on it. 'How about "Struck Striker Signs for Town"?' Jeremy was not impressed.

The day of Mark's first match duly arrived and Jeremy, though not a football fan, joined perhaps 80 others in the crowd, including 20 in the stand who had paid £3 for a seat. It was a bitterly cold day. Town were playing Westgate United who were several places higher in the league and were pressing for promotion. Jeremy found a corner of the ground, away from the biting wind, looked around, and spied Danny in the stand with a young lady he presumed to be his girlfriend, who looked cold, fed up and totally uninterested in what might be happening on the pitch. In contrast, Rachel, in the players' area, looked quite animated. Here was her husband playing in a first team game, not in the reserves.

The score was 0–0 at half time with the Town on top and Mark close to scoring more than once. With the wind at their backs, Town pressed forward and in the seventieth minute were awarded a penalty, which Carl Foster, the captain, took, but he fluffed his shot and the opposing keeper easily saved it.

Should have let Mark take it, thought Jeremy. Isn't that what he was signed for? So the game petered out to a no-score draw.

The players were glad to get to the changing room and into hot showers. There were the usual post-match congratulations and inquests. Both managers felt their team could have done better, and so on…

Rachel was there to greet Mark as he emerged from the players' entrance. It was a cold day, and a quick visit to the Crown would warm them up. Danny and Stacey, his girlfriend of only a week or two, were already there, having bagged a seat near the fire. They just about acknowledged the other couple's entrance and resumed their conversation, if it could be called that: 'Why did you bring me to this cold dump? You know I don't like football.'

'Listen, honey, it's part of my job. I've been taken on by the *Sunford Chronicle* to see if these clapped-out reporters are up to it. Jeremy is only the occasional sports guy, but I want to know what he's written. I know it was a dull 0–0 draw, but I want to "sex it up" a bit. That's what pulls in the readers.'

'Does it?' was all Stacey could reply in a monotonous tone.

Mark and Rachel acknowledged Danny and Stacey, but were thwarted by Danny's body language which said, in effect, don't sit here. So Mark and Rachel headed for the other end of the bar.

'I thought you played very well, darling,' said Rachel.

Mark replied cautiously, 'It was good to get back into first team footie.'

'Did they comment on your scar?' asked Rachel solicitously.

'No, not really, but they were certainly curious. If I'm picked next week, I guess they may well be more forthcoming!' They drove back to Manfield and were glad to get home.

Before returning to the office on Monday, Jeremy looked back on the weekend: the football and the pub on Saturday evening were OK, even if Danny and his miserable girlfriend were there. He had spent the usual boring Sunday with nothing much to do except tidy up the match report. Life was so empty and dull, the more so now that he was only working part-time. He wondered again what to do with his new free days but had little idea of how to fill the empty time.

He decided to ring his sister, Davina, but gave up when there was no reply; he was reluctant to keep feeding her answering machine. Probably at that boring old church of hers. I wonder why she bothers to go. Jeremy had no idea where, or even what, she worshipped.

'Hi, Jeremy, had a good weekend' called Danny across the office, guessing that Jeremy had spent Sunday on his own. 'Got that match report ready? The ed has asked me to read it through. OK?'

Jeremy handed it over to Danny, who was clearly enjoying his increasing power in the office.

On his now 'free' weekdays Jeremy found some DIY work to do and went for a walk, but being semi-redundant was not really his scene. He got takeaways and watched TV most evenings. Is this how life is going to be from now on? he asked himself.

On Thursday morning he now had to buy his copy of the *Sunford Chronicle* and naturally turned first to the sport on the back page.

'Mark The Mark Makes His Mark,' screamed the headline. 'Scar-faced new boy Mark Lucas led the line in Town's big game last Saturday,' the article began. 'Although he was unable to net the ball he showed many elegant touches. His lovely, sexy, wife Rachel was there urging him on (guess she is good at urging...)' Jeremy could read no more and, to the newsagent's surprise, threw it in the bin in disgust.

What had Danny done to his article, which had been written from the experience of 34 years in journalism? Is this what it came down to? he asked himself time and again. He knew in his heart that the proprietors were keeping him on just so that they could allow him to retire, and to save having to make him redundant. It was a question of costs, to a cash-strapped organisation. What was he to do?

Where could he turn? He had no other family to speak of; two cousins he had grown up with had long since ditched him. His sister was OK, but she had her own family to think of. He had some drinking associates, but could not confide in them. He felt utterly alone; his world had fallen apart in the face of a young, arrogant upstart who appeared to 'know it all'. He decided to walk round the park, which was almost empty at this time of day. He did one circuit, half admiring the flowers, and then sat on a seat. A male chaffinch hopped up almost to his feet. He looked at it, admired its lovely plumage and thought, this lovely chap hasn't a care in the world. Jeremy had never known depression but he guessed this must be similar to what it would feel like. He wanted to feed the bird standing before him with its head cocked to one side, but he had nothing on him.

Deciding to do another circuit and stop off at the café for some biscuits, he got up and started walking when his eye caught sight of a scrap of paper. Being a public-spirited sort of guy, he picked it up.

Back in his flat, Danny lay in bed with his girlfriend, who had thawed a little both emotionally and physically. Nevertheless, the relationship was not all it could be. They had known each other only a couple of weeks before she had moved in. It was an arrangement based somewhat on a rebound and on physical desire rather than love. They both knew that, but did not express it. She craved security and comfort. He just wanted sex. Or did he?

'We'd better get to work,' he muttered as he threw on his clothes. 'No time for breakfast. I'll get a coffee when I get to the office. I'm curious to see the ed's face when she reads what I've done to Jeremy's report on the match.'

With that he slammed the door, jumped into his car and drove off. He didn't see the big lorry as it hit him side on. He cared little for speed limits – they were for wimps, he would utter, or for other road users! Yes, he had six penalty points on his licence but he had only been caught twice – fair game, he would say. However, this time it was different. He was waiting at the traffic lights, impatient as ever, but actually immobile, and not with the engine revving. The lorry, out of control, careered across the lights and, on impact, scattered its load of steel pipes across the road. The driver, ashen faced, tried all he could to avoid Danny, but even at 20mph there was considerable damage. Others were soon on the scene. The fire fighters managed to cut him free, and the ambulance crew got a saline drip into his arm, but he was far from conscious. The police tried to persuade volunteers not to move the heavy steel pipes.

Other drivers were annoyed at being late for work, some were confused, and a few were in tears. The lorry driver sat slumped over his wheel while the officer in charge tried to get a statement, which proved difficult as he did not speak English. A kind paramedic helped him out of the cab and, accompanied by a police officer, took him for a check-up at the nearby hospital.

A&E were not usually busy at that time of the day but they soon had half a dozen people awaiting treatment, mainly for shock. Danny, whose life now hung by a thread, was taken to intensive care. The next few hours would tell whether or not he would survive.

Stacey, unaware of what had happened, showered, ate breakfast and rather belatedly drove to work at Welldram Building Supplies. Her boss was a tolerant soul who had got used to her late arrivals and put it down to the difficult life she was leading.

The piece of paper Jeremy had picked up read, 'Is your life in a mess? Do you want to get it sorted?' Yes, thought Jeremy, this is me. Was it religious, a joke, psychobabble or what? Obviously someone had crumpled it up and thrown it in a puddle, where only part of it had survived. Jeremy was going to bin it when he changed his mind, stuck it in his pocket and thought no more about it. Biscuits in hand, he returned to the seat, and it wasn't long before he was joined by a dozen or more feathered friends. He returned home to feed his cat. Later, his thoughts returned to the tatty piece of paper, and he had a sleepless night wondering what it meant.

Trying to establish Danny's next of kin was not easy. The staff went through his personal belongings, but it was only after the editor of the *Sunford Chronicle* rang for news of the crash and sent a reporter that it was established that his mother lived in

Preston some 200 miles away.

A&E eventually contacted her, but her response was terse and brusque. 'Serves him right, the lifestyle that he leads. No, I don't want to see him!'

The A&E Sister wondered how a mother could say that about her son. Danny's mother made a final comment. 'Try his brother, he lives nearby. Different name though. Danny changed his several years ago.' With that, the phone went dead.

The police officer in charge now delegated the matter to another officer who found, among Danny's possessions in the car, his address book. He made contact with his girlfriend via her mobile, who was immediately in a state of distress and bitterly regretted the row they had had before he left for work. She decided to visit Danny, and left work immediately for the hospital.

'It's my right,' screamed Stacey.

'I'm sorry,' said the family support officer who had now joined the conversation. 'Danny's family has first priority. I gather he has a brother somewhere near. Do you know where?'

'In Manfield,' sobbed Stacey through her tears. He has a different name, though – it's Mark, Mark Anderson. He – he – plays football.'

'You mean the chap just signed for Town. Is that Danny's brother?'

'Yes, yes, his wife is Rachel. You'll get the address from the football club.'

Mark and Rachel hurried to the hospital, produced their ID and were escorted to Danny's bedside. He was still unconscious. Mark did not know what to say. Here was his own brother lying at death's door. Tears filled his eyes as he gripped Rachel's hand. Rachel's hand gripped his even tighter.

The next day Danny was moved into the CCU as he had shown some slight improvement. Mark and Rachel had been at the bedside for about ten minutes when, to their surprise and delight, Danny opened his eyes and whispered, 'I'm sorry.'

Mark knew what he meant – how many years ago had he been slashed by his brother? Mark put his hand to his face and felt the scar. Then, to his great astonishment, Danny feebly raised his hand and touched Mark's injury. The tears flowed freely.

'Our Reporter in Terrible Crash,' screamed the headlines on the *Sunford Chronicle*. Jeremy had been called in by the editor to write the follow-up story. Work was work, and he never liked to miss a newsworthy account. He managed to get interviews with the police and a member of the A&E team, but was not allowed near the victim. Much as he disliked Danny, he felt he wanted to be near him. After all, he was a fellow journalist, or so-called journalist.

Danny eventually recovered enough to leave hospital, but would be disabled for life. Stacey had long left him for someone else. All Danny had now were his brother and Rachel, but the power of reconciliation proved a great healer. A ground-floor flat was found for Danny and adapted for his use.

Mark's career as a footballer took off and his regular goal-scoring was soon noticed by professional clubs. After two seasons with Town, he signed for a championship side some 30 miles away. From the income, they were able to purchase a better property and, with adaptations, it meant Danny could live more or less independently under the same roof. He was delighted. Not a 'Granny' but a 'Danny' flat, he was often heard to quip with a wry smile.

Rachel gave up her job and spent a lot of time with her brother-in-law, 'D' as he was now known.

'D,' said Rachel one day, 'I've got some news for you. You're going to be an uncle!'

D was again overcome. Why, why, should his brother and sister-in-law be so loving and kind when he had hurt them so much?

The compensation claim following the accident was eventually settled, which meant they could all live in some comfort.

Meanwhile, back at the newspaper, Jeremy returned to work full-time pending his eventual retirement. At home with his cat, he had recovered a good deal of *joie de vivre*. Almost every day he took out that crumpled scrap of paper. *Is Your Life in a Mess?* It was, though it had changed now that he had his old job back, albeit at Danny's expense.

He looked at his cat. 'Is your life in a mess, puss? No, not really; your needs are very simple; mine are so complicated. I'd better go and see Danny. I couldn't face it before. Yes, still in a mess, but who, or what, is going to sort it out? I can't do it on my own, I know that. Maybe the phone number on that bit of paper might help!'

The dying bishop

There was an eerie silence around the cathedral Close on the autumn evening. Bishop Cleeve lay propped up on several pillows awaiting his final hours.

Bishop Algernon Falkland Cleeve had been diocesan bishop for some 20 years, and before that archdeacon in a neighbouring diocese. He was strict, authoritarian and an expert on liturgy, and he had tried hard to maintain some order among his clergy, most of whom dutifully obeyed, though others resented his patrician stance and had as little to do with his episcopate as possible. 'Get Williamson,' he whispered. His authoritative manner had not left him yet.

Marcus Williamson was one of a succession of bishop's chaplains; some lasted only a few months, others longer, mainly because the kudos of being a 'bishop's chaplain' would look good on the CV. Marcus was no exception. He knocked timidly on the bedroom door, knowing that this inner sanctum of the palace had been out of bounds until this critical moment.

'In!' a voice intoned. The bishop rarely used the word please, and even more rarely said thank you. Williamson, dressed in his black cassock and with his prayer book clasped in his left hand, entered. 'Time to do your stuff, Williamson. You're supposed to look after my spiritual needs. God knows the others were not much good at it. What's that you've got? Hope it's a *Book of Common Prayer*. Can't stand this modern rubbish...' His words tailed off.

Williamson looked helpless. He glanced first at the nurse sitting in the corner; she remained as impassive as ever. She had seen it all before. I'm here to make sure he's comfortable. It's not real nursing but it pays the mortgage, she told herself.

Williamson then looked swiftly at Mrs Cleeve who, through the long years of a difficult marriage, had loyally supported her husband.

The bishop was not unconscious for long and was soon beckoning to Williamson. His voice, although weaker, still had at least a veneer of authority. 'Read me Matins, man, with the psalm set for the day in the Authorised Version.'

Williamson began, 'When the wicked man turneth away…'

'Enough of that,' interrupted the prelate. Williamson began again, in an even more faltering voice, 'I acknowledge my sins, my sin is ever before me.'

The bishop was only half listening. Throughout his life he had been high on the sins of others, especially his wife and family, and low on his own personal failings.

'Dearly beloved brethren, the Scripture …'

'Saying after me…' the bishop was asleep again, so Williamson recited the confession to himself. Mrs Cleeve had gone to answer the phone so, in the end, Williamson said it all, while the nurse in the corner contributed nothing, not even an impassive glance.

The phone call was from the archdeacon wanting to visit.

A few minutes after Williamson had finished, the bishop roused himself. 'Said it all, boy – didn't miss anything out, I hope?'

Williamson, who had always been afraid of anyone who spoke authoritatively, muttered, 'Yes sir!'

'If you did miss anything out, I'll know!' By now Williamson was half out of the door beating a hasty retreat, and wondering why on earth he had agreed to be the bishop's chaplain. 'Tell Mrs Cleeve I want her.'

'She's on the phone,' Williamson stammered.

'Alright, you can go,' and with that Williamson scuttled out of the room, only to be met by Mrs Cleeve on her way back to see her husband.

'It's Archdeacon Selworthy; she wants to come and see you.'

'Don't want her! Hate the woman,' was the episcopate's response. 'She's one of those evangelicals. There's a misnomer for you – an evangelical archdeacon! I know we have to have a quota of them just to keep them happy, but as an archdeacon in *my* diocese!' Gaining strength from he knew not where, he declared, 'Isn't she the one who wrote those ghastly pamphlets? What was that one called – *Is Your Life in a Mess?* I mean to say...' and his voice trailed off once again.

'Good days and bad days,' was the response of Mrs Cleeve when her sister Mavis rang, 'and today – today is one of his worst.'

'Oh dear,' was all Mavis could reply.

'Just pray it won't be long,' was Mrs Cleeve's response.

'Don't say that, dear. You've been married a long time. Don't you love him?' Mavis was full of concern.

'Mavis, we've been married more than 50 years but that doesn't mean I love him. He was domineering and a nuisance as a curate, a bully as an incumbent and a tyrant as an archdeacon and bishop – with the emphasis on *rant*.'

'Well, keep me posted,' was all Mavis could say as she rang off.

'Who was that?' the bishop demanded. 'Not that Archdeacon Selworthy again?' The bishop was awake and even more scratchy.

'No, dear, it was Mavis enquiring after your well-being.'

'Don't know why she bothers. Don't see her from one year's end to the next.'

'Yes, dear, but Mavis is very...' She knew better than to offer reasons or excuses to her irascible husband, who had now drifted off to sleep again anyway.

The phone rang again. 'Davies, diocesan secretary here.'

Mrs Cleeve, who had a soft spot for Campbell Davies, was

polite and courteous.

'I would like a minute or two with his lordship if that's at all possible.'

'I'll try. He's more likely to listen to you than anyone else.' Eventually she was able to explain to her husband that Campbell Davies would like to visit, and so it was arranged for 4pm in the afternoon.

'Five minutes, that's all.' Nurse Pargiter was at her place beside his lordship's bedside. She loved nursing, but this task was different. She had been at the bedside of many dying men and women, but this was the first time she had nursed someone as prominent (or who thought they were) as a bishop. She had a Christian faith of sorts, but in situations like this it began to waiver a little.

Campbell Davies began to explain the reason for his visit. He hesitated a little. 'Er... Um...' He had seldom been in the presence of a dying man before, let alone a prelate as powerful and pompous as Bishop Cleeve. 'The Standing Committee,' he began.

The bishop never could stand ditherers. 'Yes, they want me to resign,' the bishop said for him. 'Well, I'm not going to and that's final... and...' his voice tailed off. 'I... I...' But try as he might, his energy failed him. After a few seconds he reopened his eyes and found that Campbell Davies was still there. Regaining his strength just a little, he continued. 'Had hoped you would tell me,' he paused for breath, 'who's going to write my life.'

For more than two centuries hagiographic accounts of deceased bishops had been written on their passing to extol the achievements of their periods in office. These virtuous, weighty tomes possessed pride of place in the episcopal library. There were relatively short ones recalling the lives of such as the saintly Godson who tried to bring about change in the parishes by encouraging clergy to preach from the Bible and sought an annual retreat for the synod, but died too soon; it was said he was worn down by an unholy church. Then there was the liberal Judson who encouraged the ordination of gay clergy and largely failed in his attempts. There were numerous others, but few could match the length of service or esteem (at least in his own eyes) of Bishop Cleeve.

Campbell Davies said the wheels had been put in motion and a possible author had been approached. 'Well, who is it, man?' Like many a politician and not a few of his predecessors, Bishop Cleeve was someone who very much wanted a place in history. Not on the world scene, as kings and queens, but as a county and local figure. He cared very little for anything outside the diocese. It was as if the worldwide church never existed. He shunned the Lambeth Conference when it came round each decade. 'God's got His problems elsewhere; I've got mine here,' he would mutter from time to time.

Davies stuttered, 'We thought Selworthy would be a suitable person as she has a real gift for writing.'

The bishop had, as most people agreed, a volatile temper, and he nearly exploded. He made a feeble attempt at a shout, but it came out as a snort or a pig-like grunt. Davies thought, wrongly, that this meant a reluctant 'yes'.

So the diocesan secretary went back to his office and consulted other senior figures in the diocese. It was agreed that Sadie Selworthy should be given a month's sabbatical to produce an outline of the bishop's life. In the meantime, delicate negotiations would have to take place to obtain his lordship's approval – not that this was really needed, but in his remaining days his cooperation would be helpful, if not essential.

The private phone line, away from the bishop's office rang. 'CC here!' said a very overbearing military voice at the other end when it was answered. 'Gather his lordship's a bit off colour, what! Thought I'd pop in this afternoon, OK?' Without waiting for a reply, he rang off.

CC, or CCC as some called him, was Claude Cheverall Cleeve, the bishop's younger brother. As they were growing up they had always squabbled, and even though CC was five years younger, he was nearly always the one who gave the orders. His career initially followed a fairly predictable path, from Eton to Sandhurst – but he failed here and could only get a commission in the Catering Corps. However, he saw active service and finally reached the rank of Major (he never understood why he had not risen further as he always considered himself to be Lieutenant General, if not Field Marshall, material). He had never married. 'Not much time for women when you have a military career to think of,' was his standard remark. He'd had romantic associations, but they had always fizzled out, mainly because of his pompous attitude to life and his inability to listen to others.

CC duly arrived at lunchtime, as he always did! 'Got a spot of bother, old girl?' was his greeting on the doorstep as he gave his sister-in-law a bewhiskered kiss. The bishop's wife resented being addressed as 'old girl'. An authoritarian husband was one thing, but a bounder of a brother-in-law was quite another. Long ago she had worked out ways to manipulate the bishop, abilities which were being put to good use now he was so ill, but she had never known quite what to do with his sibling.

CC walked straight past her and made a beeline for the drinks cabinet. The bishop's spouse knew, as much as anyone else, that his promotion had been curtailed by his love of alcohol. Settled comfortably in his brother's favourite chair, he expected to be waited upon while, without so much as a by your leave, he poured himself a large whisky.

'So the old b---- is not quite tickety-boo, what?'

'He's dying,' was Gilda's stark reply as she edged toward the kitchen.

'Good Lord, didn't think it was that bad. I know the old b----has had illnesses in the past.' CC had always avoided visiting then – he thought he might catch something!

'It's only soup and sandwiches, I'm afraid,' said Gilda as she brought a tray into the lounge. 'We had ours earlier.'

'That's alright, old girl.' Gilda felt herself bridling at his description, but held her tongue. CC refilled his whisky glass, started his lunch but quickly dozed off, having mused that he could see his brother in his own good time. Other people's illnesses were jolly inconvenient, he always said. Gilda came in, collected the tray and, without disturbing him and his lunch, quietly closed the door and went back upstairs to the episcopal bedroom.

Sadie took the call and was surprised to hear that the committee would be asking her to write the bishop's biography. She was very hesitant. 'I've only written leaflets and one small booklet to help non-Christians understand what we believe,' was her immediate response.

'Look,' Campbell Davies responded, 'you may well need time to think and pray about it, but there is an urgency as the doctor thinks he has a matter of days, not weeks, to live. Shall we fix a date when you can go and see him? It won't be easy, but we think you're the person who can do the job, and do it well!'

Campbell Davies rang Gilda to say that Sadie was to write the bishop's life story, and the bishop was told. 'That woman...! that woman...' He tailed off again, although a few moments later regained his thoughts, so much so that he almost shrieked. 'She can only write those silly little books.' He was about to utter more but was unable to, exhausted as he was by his efforts.

Bishop Cleeve had fought tooth and nail against ordaining women, but had eventually conceded, declaring, 'These episcopal hands will never be laid on a woman's head,' forgetting the countless females he had confirmed during his long episcopate. When this was pointed out to him, he changed his tactics at confirmations, much to many a parish priest's lament and candidate's sadness, to simply waving his hands around the church.

One exception to this was when he visited Cleeve College, an all-boys' public school, where he did lay his hands on the boys who were being confirmed. Cleeve College was so called because the bishop had insisted on it, but thought it wise that it was named after his father whose career had been a distinguished one both in the county and further afield.

In the end, worn out by his ranting, the angry prelate fell back on his pillows exhausted. His final riposte was, 'I suppose you'll want her to come and see me. I'm not dying, you know.'

There was a long and awkward pause. Campbell Davies eventually took his leave, looked at what he perceived to be a rather pathetic figure, and left the room, to be met by Mrs Cleeve at the door. 'You know, a lot of his antipathy towards Sadie is rooted in his opposition to women in general, and the fact that she was appointed without his agreement when he was ill previously,' she said.

'Sadie Selworthy is a lovely woman. I'm sure she'll write an excellent biography,' was Campbell's farewell comment before he added, somewhat apologetically, 'It was the unanimous decision of the committee.' With that the diocesan secretary departed and the bishop's wife dutifully returned to her husband's bedside.

Finding her husband asleep and the nurse doing her crossword, Gilda appreciated the quiet in the house. CC was still dozing, so she went back to the kitchen, made a cup of tea and got out her book. She loved historical novels but had not had much chance to read anything for the past couple of weeks. She sensed that the peace of the house had something of an uneasy calm, but she could not identify the reason for her disquiet. After 20 minutes or so she silently opened the door of the lounge and saw CC slumbering still. She thought, Both brothers, neither of whom has much love for me, are out for the count! A feeling of some satisfaction crept over her which she soon dismissed with a somewhat guilty sigh. She took another look at CC and realised he had only eaten half his lunch, a meal which he had demanded an hour or so ago. The whisky glass was half full. She listened for sounds of snoring or heavy breathing, and realised to her horror that she couldn't hear any!

'Nurse!' she screamed up the stairs. 'Nurse, come at once!' Nurse did not like her concentration on the crossword interrupted, but nevertheless she did hurry down the stairs to find Gilda in no small state of distress. She felt CC's pulse and he was, in fact, lifeless. 'I'll call Dr Martin. He'll come at once. The bishop always treats him as if he were his own private physician!'

Dr Martin and the police arrived within ten minutes, and after the doctor's confirmation that CC was indeed dead, the police officer in charge, who could not have been more considerate, said, 'Just a few routine questions, Mrs Cleeve.' He remarked that it was thought possibly to have been a heart attack, but until they had access to CC's medical history and the report from Dr Martin, they had to treat it like a crime scene. He requested that nothing be touched in the room until the forensic team had completed their enquiries. They took away the whisky glass and the remains of the lunch and made a thorough examination of the room. Gilda replied to all the questions and told them all they needed to know about CC.

Within three hours Dr Martin rang to say that investigations had shown it was indeed a heart attack and that the articles taken as part of the investigation would be returned.

Gilda decided to move some of the furniture and, to her surprise, she found a letter in CC's distinctive handwriting. It read:

> Hello Big Ears, bet you thought I would never call you that again! I am writing this to ask for your forgiveness, and I know you have a good line on that subject. Forgiveness for all the hard times I have given you throughout your life. You made it, being a diocesan bishop these last 20 years, and me, what have I achieved? Major in the Catering Corps – not much, eh! Now you're on your last legs, it's time to put the record straight. Yes, we had some good times in our late teens. Do you remember Fanny, the girl from the village? Good-looking girl, what! And very easy with blokes, especially you! Remember she had a baby, a girl? What was her name? [At this point either soup or whisky had obliterated his memory.] Then she moved away and a year or so later we had to move as well. I don't know the reason, something to do with Father's status in society. You went off to Cambridge. I eventually went into the army. So we've only seen each other a few times at a wedding or two and your ordination. I remember the archdeacon saying that he had excellent candidates, whose way of life was apt and meek, etc. I could have stood up at this point, but I just laughed to myself. You were always the one who got away with things, but not now, oh no, the grim reaper has caught up with...

At this point the words tailed off.

'What was all that noise about?' The bishop had stirred himself a little as his wife entered the room.

'Oh nothing, darling,' Gilda replied, using a term she had used sparingly in their long marriage. She was on the point of telling him that CC had called, demanded his lunch, fallen asleep and then died, leaving him a note. She mused on the strangeness of the situation. Would these two brothers be buried together? Would it be half military, half ecclesiastical, and who would lead it?

Her thoughts were interrupted by the doorbell. It was Sadie Selworthy. She hurried upstairs where the bishop was obviously growing weaker. However, he did want to know a bit about her, and she recounted a little of her background – how she had never known her father, how she had studied at Durham where she had come to a living faith in Christ, how she had taught philosophy to sixth formers, trained for ordination, been a curate and vicar, but, to her surprise had been chosen to be an archdeacon. 'I think we both come from Bath.'

'Eh – yes – yes. Small world,' was all he could say.

'I would like to pray with you. Is there anything you would like to share?'

'Well, I would like to pray for forgiveness from my brother, old CC. I blamed him for getting a girl pregnant; and forgiveness from Fanny. All those years ago... could have happened to anyone.' With that his voice trailed off and he breathed his last.

Sadie thought, isn't that strange? My mother's name was Fanny.

To be continued...

Getting the paperwork done

There is a dark joke about a traffic warden who had died and was being buried. Just as his coffin was about to be lowered into the grave he woke up, knocked on the lid and shouted, 'I'm alive!' to which the vicar replied, 'Too late, I've started the paperwork!'

No organisation, company, family or individual is immune from paperwork. In spite of the vast increase in electronic communication, the amount of paper doesn't seem to reduce. The writer of Ecclesiastes 12:12 (AV) could have been speaking of such when he said, 'Of making many books, there is no end.'

Non-verbal communication of some sort or other is a part of life, whether it is a printed or hand-written, a text or an email, and so on, or whether it stands alone. For some, paperwork is a real chore, but it has to be done. Recently a man named Simon went to see a friend and was amused when he went into the loo and found a plaque with a little boy's picture and the words, 'Job's not finished until the paperwork is done!'

The destruction of written material has always been the aim of conquerors, criminals and dictators alike: consider the example of the Amorite king who destroyed Ur in 2004 BC because of its books, or the burning of the Koran by an American pastor in recent times. The written word is often seen as a threat as well as a liberator.

Despite the great and valiant efforts to translate and publish the Bible, there are still many millions of people who have no access to the Scriptures in their own language. (Of course, the worldwide web has changed a great deal.) Each new sovereign in the UK is handed a Bible during the coronation service with the words, 'It is the most precious thing this world affords.' It is doubtful that at any future coronation the new ruler will be given a CD or memory stick with the same message!

At home, Simon looked around his bookshelves, now more sparse than in recent years simply because of his many moves, but he had lined up several Bibles, or sections of them: Authorised, Good News, Blokes' Bible, *The Message* and so on, all given by well-meaning and sometimes over-enthusiastic Christian friends. He picked up one copy of the Good News version, still in pristine, unread condition, and a whole load of leaflets fell out. He was just about to bin the lot when one caught his eye. *Is Your Life in a Mess?*

He binned the others in his recycling box but stuffed this one in his back pocket. No, my life is not in a mess; it is sorted, it is untroubled, it is happy in a modest sort of way. I have no unresolved financial or emotional problems I cannot cope with, but I guess there are thousands and thousands of people who are in a hole. I'll pass it on one day to one of them.

But it remained in his back pocket for weeks and he forgot it was there. When his trousers needed cleaning, as requested by his long suffering spouse, Yvonne, he emptied the pockets and the crumpled leaflet fell out. Yvonne, ever observant, picked it up. 'I thought you weren't really into all this religious stuff.'

'No, I'm not. It's just in case I meet someone who might find it useful.'

'Humph,' she snorted as she stuffed the trousers with the other washing into the machine.

So the leaflet was left on the shelf in the utility room where it gathered dust until one day, as the back door opened, it fell on the floor. Yvonne picked it up just as Charlie, their local friendly postman, was delivering a parcel. 'Is that for me, love? I'll put it with the other mail I'm collecting to take back to the post office.' Immediately he saw it was not a letter but a leaflet.

'You can take it if you like; it's just gathering dust here,'

Yvonne replied.

So Charlie put it in the front of his van, making sure he put it face down as he did not want his supervisor questioning him about where he had got it, and even more so as to its contents. Any political or religious issues were frowned upon, especially by Mr Simpkins, his boss.

As he got out of the van, Charlie put the leaflet in his coat pocket. Later it passed into a fourth pair of hands when Myrtle noticed it in Charlie's coat.

Whatever is this? *Is Your Life in a Mess?* No, I don't think it is. Charlie and I have our disagreements but we get along fine really, she said to herself, wishing she could sound a bit more convincing. I'll take it to the play reading group this afternoon; it would be a shame to bin it, especially as it's so clearly printed and would have been expensive to produce. Nancy, who plays golf sometimes, comes along, and I'm sure she could do with some help. I don't want to judge her but she must find life tiresome, married to that old bloke who is the secretary.

Now Myrtle knew very little about golf or the local club, but she did keep her ear to the ground about local news and events.

For several months Nancy did not come to play reading, so the leaflet stayed in Myrtle's handbag. Although it had now travelled some distance, neither Simon, Yvonne nor Charlie had given any thought as to its whereabouts or, indeed, to its contents.

Looking in the bottom of her bag one day, Myrtle found the leaflet. By now it was becoming more than a little tatty round the edges. So Myrtle, who was reluctant to iron it flat, put it in a large heavy book called *Victorian Gloucestershire* which she had inherited from an aunt and which she had never opened, let alone read. So the leaflet stayed there for weeks and months, still unread.

Charlie and Myrtle decided it was time to move house, now

that the children were grown up and lived elsewhere. They found a nice two-bedroomed bungalow just two streets away and, despite the hassle and pain of leaving their old home, they agreed to purchase the new property. In no time they managed to sell their house. It had been a place of joy and no little sadness, but the decision was made. Various people came to make offers for furniture that was no longer needed, and a bookseller came to make an offer for the many unread books. Pathetic offer, thought Charlie, but they had to go. One of the books the bookseller didn't take was *Victorian Gloucestershire*.

'Nobody wants second-hand books these days,' Edgar the bookseller said as he loaded what he thought he could sell into his van, giving Charlie £30 in notes.

'What shall we do with the rest?' asked Charlie.

'Try the charity shops,' was Edgar's last comment as he closed the doors on his ancient van and drove off. So Charlie found some large, strong boxes, packed up the rest of the books and prepared to take them to a charity shop. What with all the children's old toys and other bits and pieces, the car was fast filling up, and Charlie realised the boot would not shut. He wandered off to the garage and found a dusty old bungee cord lying in the corner that he thought would do the trick. As he was fastening the boot door with it Myrtle came out to see how he was getting on, and the copy of *Victorian Gloucestershire* caught her eye.

'Oh, don't take that!' she cried. 'I was just about to read it. My Aunt Madge came from Gloucestershire.' Now the first part of the statement was not quite true, since the book had remained unread for ages, but the second part was correct.

Up until that point the stress of moving had been reasonably contained, but her comment caused Charlie to explode. 'Look, Myrtle, you've had oodles of time to read that book. You don't like large tomes, and when you do read it's more Mills & Boon than historical books.' With that he jumped into the car, slammed the door and drove off.

He was frustrated with himself for being so curt with his wife; after all, what difference would one book have made? Distracted by his thoughts, he forgot how heavy the car was but received a clunking reminder when he hit the first of several speed bumps on a local road. Everything in the car was rudely shaken up as toys fell out of boxes and a glass broke – now he had another reason to explode! He always had preferred speed cameras – why should people who keep to the speed limit have the inconvenience of these lumps in the road! If I was a councillor... he began to think as he went over the umpteenth bump, and a slightly dishevelled young man he was driving past noticed a box of books slip past the bungee cord and out of the open boot onto the road.

The young man had been out collecting cigarette ends for his morning smoke. Ever on the lookout for pickings, rich or poor, he shuffled over to the box and rifled through the pile that had been dumped in the road. He found something he thought would be useful – a big book that would prop up his bed in the squat he shared with his girlfriend Beccy. It would level up the bed nicely, he thought. Can't say I care much for the title – *Victorian Gloucestershire* – but it might impress some of my mates, even if I can't read very much; I leave that sort of thing to Beccy.

So the book found a new home, very different from its previous locations.

Sadie Selworthy settled down to write the life story of Bishop Cleeve. She was amazed that she, of all people, had been chosen. Essays at university, parish magazine articles and various leaflets were her stock-in-trade. She had, of course, visited the bishop's vast library and glanced at the tomes displayed there. They all had distinguished authors, one of whom became Archbishop of Canterbury.

She became gloomier and gloomier. The committee had impressed on her that she would be paid a reasonable sum and that they expected an outline within a month. Sadie, with a bit of hard bargaining, reminded them that she had a holiday to come as well as her responsibilities in ministry, and in the end they reluctantly extended the time to ten weeks.

The bishop's funeral was an occasion of which he would have been justly proud. It was a joint service with his brother, but CC came a poor second. However, a major from the Army Catering Corps did come and give a brief tribute. Bishop Cleeve had pride of place.

'Very fitting,' he might have said. Various dignitaries were present, including the Lord Lieutenant and other notable figures. Most of the parish clergy attended, though several came under sufferance. When the eulogies were delivered, a few held their breath, and one young curate was heard to utter, 'Blow the old s---.' Sadie felt very much out of it all. She had a small part in reading the epistle, but the bishop's family were also very much excluded. The dean was in charge, and while not a clone of the late bishop, he had always taken his lead from him. Williamson, the bishop's chaplain, was absent, having gone on sick leave.

Sadie sat down at her computer but few words would come. Just then her private phone rang. It was her mother! 'Mum, where have you been? It's ages since I heard from you!'

'Oh, I've been on one or two ocean cruises, all of which I found boring. No decent men on them.' The relationship between the two women had never been very strong. Yet there had always been more than enough money to keep them both – enough to send Sadie to boarding school at an early age and pay her way through university. Any question regarding her father or his absence was met with either blank refusal or a curt 'I'll let you know one day!'

They chatted for a while and then her mother asked, 'What are you doing? That archdeacon job seems deadly dull. You ought to get out more and meet some fellas.' It was an oft-repeated statement which Sadie chose to ignore.

'If you must know, Mum, I'm writing a biography of the late Bishop Cleeve.'

'You? You? Writing a biography? Whatever next!' The words were almost spat down the phone.

Sadie continued, 'I was asked by the diocesan secretary. I can tell you it was quite a surprise, as well as an honour.'

Sadie's mother had read the obituary of the bishop in the national press but knew no more. Sadie went on to explain the events of recent days – how CC had come to visit and died in the bishop's lounge, and there had been a joint funeral in the cathedral. There was silence at the other end of the line. Then, after a while, her mother said haughtily, 'Well, if you ask me, they got what they deserved,' and rang off.

Sadie was a little perplexed, but with the book to be written she had little time to think on her mother's peculiar behaviour. She had made a long list of the bishop's contemporaries she planned to interview, but of course there were few, if any, who had known him from childhood. The committee had given her leave of absence from her normal role, but it was proving hard to get started. She decided to pray about it all.

'Lord, here I am, a woman who has achieved some responsibility in your church. I only sought to do your will – not to achieve status or promotion – and now I've been given the daunting task of writing about someone whom I did not really know or care about. What am I going to do?' There was silence.

The phone rang and a pleasant female voice said it was S T Publishing. Sadie remembered they had published her leaflets, including *Is Your Life in a Mess?* some ten years ago, when she was just a curate. She was then put through to Jonathan who said, 'We hear you're writing the life of Bishop Cleeve and wondered how you're getting on.'

Well, that's a quick answer to prayer if ever there was one, breathed Sadie. 'Not well,' was her reply.

'Look,' Jonathan continued, 'I'll send my colleague Denis to help you if you like.'

Sadie wondered what Denis would know about the bishop but concluded that they must have an eye to publishing the material when it was eventually completed.

Denis was in his late forties, prematurely grey and of slim build. His wife had died of cancer two years earlier, leaving him with two children who were now at university. He had been in publishing all his life. He even saw it as something of a vocation to help budding authors. He rang later that day. 'Come and have some lunch,' Sadie invited.

So they duly met, and she found Denis very easy company. He talked about structure, ways to keep the reader interested, drama, tension, family background and so on. In the end Sadie had a pile of useful notes, and the meeting had indeed proved to be an inspiration, even if the subject matter of a pompous old bishop did not inspire her in the least. She would have much preferred to write something to help people in their Christian faith.

Denis duly thanked her for the meal. He had never met an archdeacon before, let alone eaten with one, and a female one to boot. He came from a tradition where women ministers were only tolerated, and not in 'headship', as he called it. Nevertheless, as he was getting into his car he said, 'It's been lovely meeting you, Sadie. I... I... would like to see you again. Would you mind?'

Sadie was staggered. It was years since she had had any sort of relationship with a fellow. She felt she had been called to the single life of service. 'Well, er... yes,' was all she could utter. Here was the super-confident archdeacon in a real fix: how to write a difficult book and how to behave towards Denis.

Within a day Denis had rung and they agreed to meet at the Sygon Arms in Framlington about 15 miles away. Sadie was sure that would be 'out of range', as it were, of the prying eyes of any diocesan officials. What should she wear? Obviously not her clerical attire; something feminine, but not too over-the-top.

They enjoyed a lovely meal, which Denis insisted on paying for, and found themselves very easy in each other's company. Sadie said a bit about her background: a first in English at university, becoming a Christian there as well, the call much later to ordained ministry, and not least, the sadness in her life of not knowing her father, no siblings and a cool relationship with her mother who had rung so recently. Denis recounted something of his past life, and how he had got into publishing.

'This bishop chap, were there no redeeming features in his life? He seems to have been shipped straight out of Barchester Towers! You might find out more about him than you think.' They agreed on a programme of interviews, beginning with Mrs Cleeve, in order to provide an outline in time for the committee's deadline.

What a super guy, thought Sadie, and without any hesitation they agreed to meet each other the following Saturday, at Denis' home. Was it remiss of her to think she felt 20 years younger? As they were going to the car park they were approached by a young couple, scruffily dressed.

"Ere, look, we don't want none of your money,' said the young man, 'but would you like this book?' Sadie and Denis were taken aback. It looked like a large antique volume.

'Well, I don't know,' was their joint response.

The young man continued, 'You see, I can't read very well, and Beccy here says it's quite boring.'

Denis was quick on the uptake since his knowledge of books knew few boundaries. 'Yes, I'll take it. Here's £20 for it.'

As he was handing the money over, a leaflet fell out. It was *Is Your Life in a Mess?* Sadie picked it up and gave it back to the young couple. 'You keep this,' she said, 'and by the way, I was the one who wrote it!'

'You did?!' shouted the young couple in unison.

'I'll sign it if you like,' and before she could open her handbag, Denis had produced a pen with which Sadie signed with a flourish, 'With love in Christ, Sadie Selworthy'.

'Let's find a corner in the pub and read it together,' said Beccy as they walked off.

'But I can't read,' mumbled Jason.

'But I can; I'll read it to you,' said Beccy, 'and who cares if others hear!'

It was a beautiful sunny, spring day. Sadie and Denis, with his son Dermot as best man and Suzy his daughter as bridesmaid, were married in the packed cathedral. The choir prepared to sing their hearts out, though the choirmaster was not familiar with some of the songs of worship, especially those chosen by the bride and groom. Devon practised hard on the drums for the newly formed music group. The dean was nowhere to be seen as he had gone on pre-retirement leave. The new bishop, dressed smartly but casually, was beaming from ear to ear.

Sadie had decided not to be 'given away' but rather to process down the long aisle with Denis by her side. As they entered the great west door, they were met by a smiling Beccy and Jason. They looked so different. There was no chance to say anything, but the words 'Thank you' were written all over their faces.

The second surprise Sadie had was to see her mother, elegantly attired, waiting for her. Feelings welled up as they greeted each other.

'Don't, Sadie! My expensive mascara will run!'

'So will mine,' exclaimed Sadie. 'Oh, how I wish my father

had been here to give me away. Oh, I so wish he could have been here!'

Her mother replied, 'He is here, darling. Look over there.' And they both turned towards the tomb of the late Bishop Cleeve.

The invigilator

He paced up and down, occasionally pausing to look over a candidate's shoulder to see what they were writing. His eagle eye was on the lookout for any possible cheating or illegal use of mobile phones. Not that he had ever caught anybody, but the university regulations were quite clear. Now and again he glanced out of the window where the sun was shining; one or two office workers were sunbathing and several couples were enjoying a picnic.

Why does he do it? Is it the power and control? Is it the pay – pay for being bored? Is that it? He had retired from teaching in a secondary school four years previously where he had ended his career as deputy head. He had applied for various head teacher's posts but had only ever been shortlisted once, and had to settle for what he considered second best.

The advert was a very small one: 'Invigilators required. Applications from former teachers particularly welcome. Training given.'

'What training do I need?' he snorted, but nonetheless applied, and passed the aptitude and security checks, and now here he was with more than two hours to go.

Goodness knows how many miles I'll walk today, he thought. Five or six or maybe more – who knows? He could have opted for the post with individual students in their own homes. The university had pioneered a system where candidates who had some form of disability, such as dyslexia, and who would be disadvantaged by sitting among a larger number of candidates, could be allowed to sit in familiar surroundings. He thought that would be too much one-to-one contact and he'd had enough of that at school. This was OK. It provided some pocket money – not that he needed it: his educational and state pensions were plenty for his needs. His ground-floor flat needed little maintenance. He rarely watched TV and amused himself by listening to his classical CDs (he had more than 500) and reading, mainly historical novels.

His one adventure, if it could be called such, was the Philatelic Society, which he enjoyed. He always resisted persuasive attempts to elect him to the committee, even though he could see they were short of people.

Such was his life. Some might say it was humdrum, but it suited him. An only child, he had never sought out human company. He had had brief female relationships in his younger days but they never developed.

He had concluded, long ago, that marriage was not for him. School had occupied most of his waking hours. Summer schools with history and philately occupied the holidays. He avoided the bar at summer schools and always retired to his room after dinner.

He had been on tours to see some of the classical sites such as Florence, Athens and Rome. He made a point of reading as much as possible about the places he was going to visit. It meant, so he thought, that he could be as knowledgeable as the tour guide and, should anyone ask him, he could give an authoritative answer. The trouble was that nobody did ask him, so his newly acquired knowledge was kept to himself. He didn't bother with people and they rarely bothered with him. All this was very much in the back of his mind.

'Why am I doing this?' he asked himself. The conclusion he came to, at least in part, was that he wanted to keep in touch with the world of education.

Suddenly his musings were interrupted by the sight of a silver head at a desk in the front row. His colleague had checked the candidates in so he had not really taken much notice of them, but this one looked different to the usual 'types', at least from above. He had no chance to see her face as she bent diligently over her desk, writing her answers in a careful methodical script. He guessed she must be in her late fifties but found it difficult to tell. He tried not to pause but hesitated for a second in his perambulation just enough to see her look up and smile at him – a smile that dazzled him and, for a micro second, he forgot his role and smiled back. He was glad that his colleague was preoccupied in other matters and did not notice. People rarely smiled at him, and certainly not females of a certain age.

When the exam was over the candidates laid their answer books on their desks and he and his colleague collected them, packaged them in the correct manner and announced to the candidates that they were free to leave. Thank goodness that's over for another year, he thought. A courier was waiting at the door ready to collect the parcels. He signed various forms to say the exam had been conducted in accordance with the university regulations and retrieved his coat and briefcase. Why he brought his briefcase he had no idea, but it helped with the image!

He walked to his smart car and was just about to drive off when he saw her sitting in a vehicle opposite, doing something on her mobile phone. The autumnal sun shone through the trees, and her silver hair reflected it in a way that struck him quite strangely. She looked up and smiled and, before he knew it, he had crossed the car park towards her car. She wound down the window as he approached.

'How did it go?' he enquired. It was a question he had never ever dared to ask a candidate before, either in his teaching days or now as an invigilator.

Still, there was nothing in the rules to say he could not speak to a candidate after the exam. She smiled her dazzling smile again. 'OK,' she said in a somewhat slurred manner. He thought, heavens, she's intoxicated or drunk! But then recovered himself in double-quick time, realising that she was deaf and that she relied on being able to lip-read. He further deduced that she had sat at the front so that she could lip-read the instructions for the exam.

In no time at all she had offered him a peppermint from a packet she kept in the car, which he accepted very happily. People offered him very little these days; even a peppermint was a small joy for so lonely a man. 'Thank you,' he said, slowly and deliberately, mouthing the words.

She smiled, and then very deliberately said, 'Goodbye,' but in such a way that signalled she hoped they would meet again. On such small things all sorts of future events might depend, such is the nature of random or chance encounters.

Just then he noticed a man sitting in the back seat, working on his laptop. The silver-haired lady introduced him. 'This is Lionel.'

'Hi!' came a voice from within the car. He also noticed that the female candidate was sitting in the driving seat of the car.

How can you drive a car when you are completely deaf? he wondered, and then realised it was a left-hand drive vehicle; a quick glance told him it was an American model.

'Lionel Trimbone,' said an American voice. 'Here's my card.' It said:

LIONEL T TRIMBONE
Real Estate
2417 Rio Grande Avenue
Albuquerque
New Mexico 837912

'At school I was called Tommy Trombone, but I never got round to playing. Did she do well?'

'It's not for me to say. I'm only there to ensure fair play, not mark the papers. They've all been sent off to the examiner at the university.'

'You don't say,' said Lionel. 'Look, we must be going.'

He moved into the driving seat and drove off into the autumn sunshine. So this female candidate, for whom he had fleetingly felt a slight attraction, was Mrs Trimbone. Time to forget and go back home, he thought. Certainly, he thought, anything like further involvement would not be countenanced by the university authorities anyway. He went back to his car which, to his horror, he found he had left unlocked, but was relieved to find nothing amiss. As he got in he turned over Lionel's card. On the reverse it read, 'Lionel T Trimbone, UK address and office, The Barns, Frandingham, Glos. GL94 07U. Email LTT@uk.phonemail.co.uk Mobile 70777 794851.'

So he knew where she might live. Frandingham was only seven miles away. He wondered whether she was American too. Because of her impeded speech it was hard to tell. Perhaps she was British and married to an American, but how could she study properly if she spent so much time in the USA?

Back home he looked up Albuquerque in his world atlas. It said, 'City in central New Mexico, pop. 450,000, situation 5,000 feet above sea level.' How on earth does a deaf, not unattractive woman from New Mexico become a mature student in West Gloucestershire? he wondered. How does anybody become anything? Perhaps she was bored having her husband so many thousands of miles away for much of the time.

His musings were interrupted by the doorbell ringing. He was not expecting a visitor so opened the door with some curiosity. He was more than surprised to see a police officer standing there and enquiring if he could come in. He opened the door wider and invited him into his lounge which, although sparsely furnished, was not uncomfortable.

'I wonder if you could help us, Sir?' enquired the PC.

'I will if I can,' he replied, feeling somewhat perplexed.

The officer explained that there had been a nasty accident

where a car had collided with a lamp post and the occupants had been badly injured, one very seriously. 'We believe you met the occupants at the Civic Hall car park earlier.'

He realised to his horror that the people involved were the Trimbones. He then explained that he had been an invigilator at the exam, had chatted with them in the car park afterwards and had been relieved when he realised that the woman was not going to be driving as he had discovered she was deaf. The officer did not comment but instead asked, 'Don't you get bored pacing up and down for such a long time? How long is it?'

'Three hours, Officer, and yes and no,' he replied. 'It can't be too different from you walking the beat.'

'Afraid we don't do much of that these days, Sir.'

He replied to the policeman's further questions saying that Mr Trimbone had given him his business card and that was all. 'I'm afraid I can't be of much more help to you. How did it happen?'

'Well, it was a left-hand drive car, which may have had some bearing on the matter. He had more serious injuries, but she, too, was badly hurt.'

The news of the Trimbones was not very good and, contrary to his nature, he said, 'I would like to go and see them if possible.' Hospitals were not places he exactly warmed to – 'factories for the dying,' he had heard it said, and he felt in agreement. Having apologised again that he could not be more helpful, he said goodbye to the officer.

He went to the bus stop and travelled to the hospital. The helpful red-coated volunteer told him it was not visiting hours and that outside these times access was very restricted. He explained that he was the last person to speak to them prior to the crash and that he wondered whether a brief visit might help. He found the ICU ward but discovered that the Sister was not very sympathetic. Her first consideration was the well-being of her patients, which was right and proper. She said Mr Trimbone was unconscious and that a visit would not be possible. Moreover, the chaplain was with him.

'What does a chaplain know about medicine?' he thought, as he made his way out of the ward. As he was leaving, the chaplain and a doctor came out. Their faces did not look encouraging. He enquired of Lionel Trimbone and explained that although he was not a relative, he was the last person to speak with him before the accident. He was told that he had died a short while ago.

Help! he thought. Will it be my job to break the news to her?! He explained the situation and his role in it all to the chaplain, who said he would go ahead and break the news to her. He already knew that she was profoundly deaf and that he would need to use all his skills to communicate with her so that she could lip-read.

What should he do now? His first thought was to run out of the hospital as soon as he could. He loathed the place. How could people work there? Instead, he headed for the café, ordered a coffee and sat down to think. Should he go and see Mrs Trimbone? He was not good at difficult situations and had avoided them like the plague when he was teaching. It had been bad enough telling Mrs Saxelby next door that her cat had been run over, but this was very different. Oddly, he felt like praying, even though it wasn't really his thing, and certainly not with all these people here in the café. Perhaps there was a chapel. If there was a chaplain there must surely be a chapel. He supposed they would have such a place in a hospital. He made enquiry of a couple of porters having a break.

'Feeling a bit holy, are you?' said one.

'It's down the corridor on the right,' chipped in the other, more helpfully.

And so it was, in a state of limbo and shock, that he found the entrance to the chapel. Comfy chairs, he thought to himself.

Might stop here for a while. Lionel's dead, and presumably after the inquest he'll be taken back to the USA for a funeral. But what about his wife? Will she be fit enough to travel?

'Pippa's going to be OK and should be able to go home tomorrow,' a voice said. He turned round and found that it belonged to the chaplain. 'She indicated that she'd like to see you.'

Now he was faced with another dilemma. Here was a woman in shock and bereaved, a woman he hardly knew and with whom he was likely to have difficulty communicating. Was she seeking his help, and if so why?

'It's make up your mind time!' He recalled himself saying that to hundreds of hesitant children who were dithering over trivial things, especially the girls in the fifth form.

He went to the hospital shop, bought a bunch of flowers and headed to the ward, receiving strange looks from some in the lift, not realising the reason. He walked in, without seeing the sign which read, 'Please Do Not Bring In Flowers'.

He saw her in a chair, looking out of the window. He hesitated for a moment, then pushed them over her shoulder, before any of the staff could object. 'These are for you, Pippa.'

'How very kind!' She had not only heard, but answered him quite normally as well. By this time the ward sister had arrived; she completely ignored the flowers and said, 'Praise the Lord – it's a miracle!' Conversation just flowed between them all.

Eventually Pippa said, 'Lionel will be taken back to Albuquerque for burial. Will you come?'

'Why, er... er... yes,' was all he could manage to say.

The service at the mega city church was attended by hundreds. They came not just to pay their respects to Lionel but also because they wanted to hear a clear message about God's hand in it all. Pastor David said a lot – perhaps too much! At one point he made a play on Lionel's surname, at which the four trombones in the orchestra played a lovely item in tribute.

The minister concluded by saying that out of one man's death a miracle had occurred – Pippa could now hear and speak. Loud applause echoed round the church. Pippa stood up and thanked everyone, saying it was through Jesus that miracles still occurred.

'Lionel's sister has shown such courage.' Lionel was stunned to hear one of the congregation call her Lionel's sister.

Sister? Sister? I thought she was Lionel's wife! Then by way of confirmation, he realised that the family sitting across the aisle were Lionel's wife and children. He felt very confused and somewhat alone.

After she introduced him to them and to various other friends and family, including Pastor David, Pippa said she must stay in the USA for a while, but then she would be coming back to England to live.

So he caught various connecting planes and arrived back at Gatwick two days later. The flights gave him plenty of time to think about all that had happened.

Weeks later, Ryley bought fish and chips and noticed that the outer wrapping was a recent copy of the local paper and, although the cooking oil had soaked through, he could see the headline 'Miracle Woman to Wed Former Teacher'. He saw the accompanying photograph and thought, surely 'Old Crusty Fusty', as we used to call him, can't be getting married! The rest had been obscured, but he had seen enough to text his old school mates with the news.

A fortnight after they were married, a brown envelope dropped through the door of their new home. It was addressed to 'Miss P Trimbone'. She tore it open excitedly, only to read, 'We regret to inform you that you have failed to gain the requisite marks in your exam…'

She read no further but threw it down on to the floor and, finding her husband, put her arms around him. 'That'll teach me to concentrate on the exam questions and not on the invigilator!'

He could only wonder about it all and remember Lionel, and the pastor's words, 'Out of one man's death, a miracle has occurred.' And he thought, that might just include me as well.

Visitors to the vicarage

Simon and Yvonne Hawse lived in the vicarage, only it had not been a proper vicarage for many years. The vicar, the Rev Penny Black, lived in a modern house in Framlington, some three miles away. Simon had once received a letter from a body calling itself The Church Commissioners saying it was not considered good practice to continue calling the property 'The Vicarage' and suggesting names like Glebe House, or Pastures New, but he binned it, as he did many letters with which he did not agree or which offered him unsolicited advice. Yvonne suggested calling it 'The Vyecarage'. 'Too much a reminder of your late mother,' was Simon's response. His late mother-in-law had been called Violet, and he had long and painful memories of her.

They both enjoyed the status of a six-bedroomed house which they had extensively modernised. While not exactly having 'Lord of the Manor' standing, they felt drawn into the stream of upward social mobility. Hawse Reclamation Holdings had done well since its humble beginnings some 30 years earlier. They had toured every scrapyard for miles around, visited countless car boot sales and acquired all sorts of very old, if not antique, items, such as fireplaces and cast-iron stoves, for which, in due time, they found a ready market. Now they employed 16 people, three-quarters of whom were engaged in restoration work in their modern warehouse on the nearby industrial estate. The remainder were out on the road looking for suitable materials. Simon, in addition to being managing director, now did searches and research for discerning customers who wanted specific items such as wooden balustrades of eighteenth- or nineteenth-century origin. He had now built up a sufficient client base to be quite choosy about those for whom he worked.

Simon enjoyed all the trappings that a successful businessman would expect to enjoy. With their corporate entertaining, Hawse Reclamation Holdings sponsored cricket at the local ground, as well as other events that afforded good publicity. Soon invitations arrived to join Rotary and Freemasons. 'Good for contacts and your image, old boy!' declared one of his customers. He declined, since he was now in a position where he could pick and choose with whom he wanted to mix. However, he did apply to join the local golf club. He knew there was a waiting list so did not expect to hear anything for some while. 'Waiting for dead men's shoes,' he called it and, seeing how slowly some of the players took to play their rounds, he wondered whether some of them might not already be. However, he was occasionally asked to play a round as a guest. William Bates (he had dropped the nickname 'Bill' years ago), an ex-builder whose contacts were more than useful, had invited him. Simon had enjoyed himself, but it was not the same as being a member. Then, much to his surprise, William whispered in his ear, 'Fixed it for you, lad.'

'Fixed what?' replied Simon in surprise.

'Why, membership, of course!' Simon was taken aback, but delighted nevertheless. William had the philosophy in life that everyone was open to being bribed which, although not completely true, was one that he relentlessly pursued. 'Money talks,' he added, with a nod and a wink.

In due course, Simon's application was approved by the club committee and his membership card posted to him.

Other trappings of success came his way. He wanted to acquire a personalised number plate. He thought of HRH 1 for himself and HRH 2 for Yvonne, but that was impossible. Eventually he had to settle for HRH 666 for himself and HRH 667 for his wife. The Merc and her 1950s Jaguar sports car looked beautiful in the driveway. They made sure one of the staff cleaned them at the warehouse – they did not want to be seen cleaning their own cars! Of course, they left them outside at home as much as possible to impress passing motorists, pedestrians and the inquisitive neighbours.

Sadly, there were two disappointments. The first was that there were no children. When the curious Violet used to enquire of her daughter about this she was told that much as they would like to have children, they were too busy.

'Too busy for sex? I don't believe it!'

However that was all many years ago. The other disappointment was more of a nuisance in that people would knock on the door wanting the vicar. Simon considered impersonating one and putting on a funny voice. The only vicar he knew of was the Rev Penny Black, and that was merely a passing acquaintance, sharing just a quick greeting on Remembrance Sunday each year; Simon never forgot that his grandfather was killed on D-Day. But the biggest difficulty with the house being mistaken for a genuine vicarage was when people wanted money or food. He and Yvonne would explain that it was no longer a vicarage and callers should try the Rev Black at Framlington.

However, one Saturday morning, a smartly dressed man named Sam arrived, saying that he only wanted food, not money. 'You are not the vicar,' he said, in a gentle, educated voice when Simon opened the door. Simon explained who he was and that it was no longer an ecclesiastical property. 'May I ask your name?' he continued.

'I'm Samuel Shoneggar. I've been on the road for years. I'm German, originally from Hamelin.' At this, Simon's ears pricked up; his great-grandfather had come from a part of Germany where Shoneggar was a common name. Indeed when Simon's grandfather was called up in 1943, the recruiting sergeant questioned his British credentials. Simon, however, had always identified himself as British, and enjoyed the minor status of a name that was unusual.

Mr Shoneggar, emphasising the 'Mr', explained that he had been a language teacher in France until a few of the locals objected to him teaching at 'their' school. They had bitter memories of Nazi atrocities in their town during the war, hence there was some residual anti-German feeling. So Mr Shoneggar was unable to get a job despite his considerable language skills. He came to Britain and, while he could not detect any anti-German prejudice as such, he had still been unable to get a job, so had drifted around and had kept out of trouble, but life on the road was all he now knew.

Simon was fascinated. Is this what all vicars get on their doorstep? he thought. Glad I'm not one!

Just as Sam was leaving, Yvonne swept into the drive in her sports car. Simon called out, 'Hello darling.'

Without responding she cried out, 'Who on earth was that?'

'Just a guy who wanted some food.'

'You didn't give him any?!' she cried, aghast.

Simon said, 'Well, he had an interesting story to tell, and he comes from the same part of Germany as my great-grandfather.' Yvonne was not impressed but decided to let the matter drop, resolving to make sure anyone else who called did not receive the same undeserved hospitality. But they still came. There was Frank, the ex-soldier with a broad Cornish accent, who offered to do odd jobs but declined when Simon suggested manual work such as cutting hedges. Frank eyed the gleaming Merc and offered to clean it, much to Simon's disgust. Car cleaning was done at the warehouse and not in his drive! Then there were Larry and Joe, asking for money as well as wanting food.

Why, Simon asked himself, is it only Saturday mornings? He usually played golf in the afternoons. Why did they always call when Yvonne was at her ladies' coffee circle at the golf club?

Yvonne's take on it was, 'I expect they have a secret communication system showing you're a soft touch. Denise at the club says there are probably marks on the road saying this house is OK.'

Sure enough, after searching for half an hour, they found a mark which said 'SA.AM.OK'. It was very faint. 'I'll bet Mr Shoneggar did that months ago,' was Yvonne's comment, and she resolved to change the situation. If Simon would not say no to these uninvited guests, perhaps she should call the police. But, on reflection, she felt that would not solve the problem. She crept into Simon's garage to get a chisel to scratch out the mark, but before she could find one there was another knock on the door. This time it was no tramp, but a police officer.

'Come in. Can we offer you a cup of tea?'

'No thank you,' he replied. Simon and Yvonne wondered why he had come. He explained that Joe had been found dead in Farlington Park, and they had arrested three of his homosexual friends on suspicion of murder. They all denied it, but admitted indecent acts in a public place. One of them declared that Joe had told them the old vicarage in Little Badfield was a place to get food.

Simon and Yvonne were indeed very shocked, and explained the situation to the officer. Yvonne even went on to say she had contemplated calling the police over these unwanted visitors. The officer took a statement and was shown the marks outside the house. He said there was no more they could do to help the investigation and that they would not be needed further.

From then on the visits became fewer and fewer, and Simon decided to play golf on Saturday mornings while Yvonne was 'caffeining', as she called it, among her female friends.

Christmas was fast approaching. When the day arrived, Simon and Yvonne enjoyed it on their own. 'All our friends have their families so we enjoy each other's company,' they declared, though without great conviction.

However, 'Twixmas' was the highlight of their social year, when they invited the golf club committee to a party at their home. It was a black-tie do. Yvonne had been preparing for weeks, although she actually employed a caterer to prepare the food. Most of the guests thought she had produced it all herself. She did not disillusion them. 'Oh, Yvonne, you have been busy, and so near Christmas. I don't know how you manage to do it!' they cooed.

Yvonne smiled what she thought was her most convincing smile and said, 'Oh, it was nothing really!'

Simon, meanwhile, was dispensing a wide variety of aperitifs. The president arrived alone saying, 'I'm between wives at the moment.' Looking for a fourth, no doubt, thought Simon as he poured him a large Martini. Other members drifted in with a variety of spouses and 'other attachments'.

The secretary arrived with his charming wife, Nancy. 'Do you fancy Nancy?' whispered the president in Simon's ear. Simon did not reply but did make a beeline for her, a move not unnoticed by Yvonne as she hurried with dishes from the kitchen.

In all, 25 people were present. The size of the rooms allowed plenty of space for them to mingle and to congregate in small groups around the table that held the huge buffet meal. Simon made sure people had full glasses. A few stuck to fruit juice or non-alcoholic drinks, but others said, 'Blow it, it's Twixmas. The police only look for drunk drivers over Christmas and New Year.'

The president, having failed to make any impression on the charming Nancy, said to Simon, 'Can I have a look round? I've never been in a vicarage before.'

'OK,' said Simon, making sure the guests were being looked after by Yvonne. The president had a quick survey of the house.

Peering through the curtains he said, 'What's that out the back?'

'That's the start of the swimming pool,' said Simon.

'Great!' replied the president. 'We can all enjoy it when you invite us again in the summer!' Now, inviting the golf club committee in the summer was the furthest thought from Simon's mind. 'Any trouble getting planning permission?'

'No, I haven't actually got it yet, but William gave me a decent quote and I wanted to get started. He said he knows enough people on the planning committee to get permission, even if retrospectively. It seems William Bates can fix anything and everyone, for a price.'

'A useful man to have in the club!' replied the president. 'I'll try and chat to him later. By the way, I hear you have your fair share of uninvited visitors. Rather you than me. I hear that gay fellow who was murdered in the park had come here. Did the *Chronicle* send a reporter to see you? I hope it wasn't that upstart in a motorised wheelchair – Danny something-or-other, I think his name is. I can't stand him.'

But before Simon could reply or even comment on the people who called, the president was off in vain pursuit of another female conquest.

Just then there was a ring on the doorbell. Simon wondered who on earth it could be at this time of night – a gatecrasher? He called Yvonne, who was serving desserts, to come quickly as there was someone at the door. They made a rapid assessment to make sure none of the guests had been left out in the cold and was returning, so decided it could only be gatecrashers. They were too far from neighbours for it to be anyone complaining about noise.

'Someone is going to spoil our Christmas,' shouted Yvonne.

'Well, don't just stand there – let's see who it is.' Simon picked up a wooden mallet that had been left in the hall, just in case, and they opened the door. They were more than surprised to see a young couple standing there. She was perhaps 17, if that; he looked a good deal older. They were certainly of Middle Eastern origin (probably illegal immigrants, was Simon's first thought). Then he noticed the girl was cradling a baby, a very young baby, which she tried to offer to Yvonne.

'Ow my Gawd,' cried Yvonne, but not loud enough to be heard above the party noise. 'Ow my Gawd,' she repeated.

'Probably is,' said Simon softly.

The tumuli

'Are we nearly there yet?' Sophie was tired and bored. Nine-year-old Sophie and her seven-year-old brother Freddie had occupied the back seat of the ancient Volvo, which her mother had borrowed from her grandmother, for what seemed like years. The destination was Lyme Regis. Sophie loved the town, not because of its scenic location or its history, but because it had a nice beach not far from their usual guest house, and she loved walking along The Cobb and watching fishing boats coming in and out of the harbour.

'What are those, Mummy?'

'They're tumuli, darling.' Sophie was none the wiser.

Steve was staying with the family for a while. He didn't like children, and the feeling was mutual. He decided not to enter into the conversation, a stance he would adopt for most of the coming week. Steve was a man of few words – something that Felicity found quite mysterious. She tried to explain from behind the steering wheel as she coped with the holiday traffic that tumuli were put up by Bronze Age people to bury their dead.

'Why?' Sophie was not satisfied as they passed another couple of ancient sites. 'When Granny died she went to the crematorium.'

'Well, they didn't have crematoria in those days.' Felicity was doing her best to satisfy the child's curiosity.

'Why two together?' Sophie was not to be fobbed off. 'Is there only one person in each, or lots and lots of bones?'

'Look, when we get to Lyme Regis we'll go to the museum and see if they have any information on tumuli!'

Sophie still persisted. 'There are only a couple together;

looks like one of those road signs – you know the ones – Dad says they look like a woman lying in the road.'

'Well, your dad isn't here.'

'Wish he was. Don't like *him*,' Sophie blurted out, indicating Steve. Steve, in the front seat, ignored the comment and stared ahead.

'Will I get bumps on my chest when I'm older?' Conversations in a noisy car with a driver frustrated by the queuing traffic and a questioning child behind are never easy, and this was no exception.

'Yes you will, dear. All women have them.'

'Don't want them. Want to stay as I am,' was the curt reply as they entered the outskirts of Bridport. All thoughts about ancient burial mounds receded rapidly from the child's mind. At the traffic lights Freddie awoke with a start and wondered where he was.

'Can we stop for an ice cream?' Sophie was more interested in refreshment than in arriving at her holiday destination.

'All right, I'll try and find a shop.' Parking in Bridport was not easy at the best of times, but they managed to find a space in the main street. Soon they were on their way again. Steve had said very little on the journey, even though Felicity had tried hard to engage him in conversation.

Their meeting had been rather odd. Dyke, her husband, had left her a couple of months into their tenth year of marriage, saying he was 'fed up with married life'. She had pleaded with him to stay especially for the sake of the children, but he was firmly resolved to leave and found himself a flat a mile or so away. Felicity was distraught and tried to explain to the children carefully what had happened.

'Why doesn't Daddy love us any more?' was Sophie's angry outburst, and Felicity did her best to help them understand, but for many nights the children cried themselves to sleep.

Felicity rang her best friend, Zoe, who had babysat several

times in the past and had been a single mum for many years. Widowed at 27, her husband Guy had not left her for another woman but had succumbed to cancer. Zoe was full of concern.

'Look F' – Felicity preferred 'F' to her full name – 'why don't you all come to Skids Club on Monday week? It runs every week except half term. You'll enjoy it. "Skids" stands for Special Kids, 'cause all kids are special. You'll find plenty of girls in the same situation as yourself.'

'I don't feel I can meet anyone socially at the moment,' was all Felicity could mumble. 'Anyway, isn't it run by some kind of church? I don't want my children to be affected by religion.'

'Well,' said Zoe after a pause, trying to choose her words carefully. 'It is run by members of the church, but they don't preach at you. They're just a friendly crowd who have the best of intentions for the children and their parents at heart.'

There was a long pause. Eventually Zoe said, 'Look F,' – 'Look F' was always her opening gambit when she was being serious – 'come just once and see what you think.'

'No, I have a job interview. Now that Dyke has gone I have to restart my life on my own. He does give me an allowance, which is enough, but I have to get back to my career.'

'Alright, but what about Tuesday?' Another long pause ensued, and eventually Zoe said, 'OK, look F. I'll take care of the kids while you go for the interview and we will go to the Skids Club with Sophie and Freddie on Tuesday. Meanwhile, let's go for a bit of retail therapy before the children come home from school.'

'Retail therapy' was the last thing on F's mind, but she did look at some clothes in a department store, even though her mind was in a whirl. Should she obtain Dyke's permission to take the children to Skids Club or not?

Zoe put her mind at rest. 'He's gone, and they're your responsibility now.'

Café Noir beckoned and they ordered two lattés.

'F, this is my treat. We'll do something a bit more substantial next week.'

As they made their way to the car park they met a young man selling *The Big Issue*. 'Like to buy a copy, ladies?' He was about 5'10" tall, of slim build and in his mid-twenties.

'Er, OK, yes,' said F hesitantly.

'I'll buy it,' said Zoe. 'You can pass it on when you've read it.'

'Thank you, ladies.' The man's deportment and accent suggested an educated background, and were in direct contrast to his dress and surroundings. F couldn't help noticing his unlikely demeanour.

She was home in time for the children's return and to hear their stories of school, and their excitement at breaking up for half-term, and she soon forgot the man she had met in the street. However, after the children had gone to bed she remembered the *The Big Issue* seller and Zoe's kindness, and she wondered what her future held. Was there to be one? It did not seem as if there was much hope of it, despite the prospects of a job after the weekend.

Saturday morning dawned bright and clear and Dyke called to take the children to the park. Nothing was said between the parents, and the children, still feeling very puzzled, went, somewhat reluctantly, with their father. They enjoyed the time on the swings, but they had no understanding why Mum and Dad were living separately.

F, on the other hand, was still puzzled by *The Big Issue* seller, and she found herself thinking how his life must have taken an unexpectedly tough turn just as hers had. The future suddenly seemed so difficult and uncertain. Why was he there? Why was he homeless? *Was* he homeless? Where did he live? Where did he come from? These and hundreds more questions came into her mind. She had a couple of hours to spare so she caught the bus – Dyke had said he needed their car – and went into town.

'Looking for someone?' a tall, well-built lady enquired.

'Well, yes, actually.' F was quite taken aback. 'I was looking for the guy who sells *The Big Issue*.'

'On Saturdays he goes to a pitch outside the railway station. He reckons on better sales there than on weekdays. He won't be difficult to find. Good luck.' But she muttered under her breath, 'Don't know why she should bother. They're all scroungers.'

There he was, with *The Big Issue* in his right hand and a smile on his face, offering the magazine to a man in a smart suit who was obviously off to some sort of function – maybe a wedding. The suit thought very little of *The Big Issue* sellers and was beginning to harangue him when he realised his train was due and left mid-sentence.

Steve seemed a little shaken when Felicity spoke to him. 'Excuse me, but I've come to see you. I don't know really why, but I'm fascinated by what you're doing. Have you been selling *The Big Issue* for long?'

Steve gave her a cautious look and, in response to her invitation, agreed to go for a cup of coffee in a nearby cafe. They sat down and he began to talk, albeit in a rather hesitating manner. He was surprised that someone was caring about him – or at least there appeared to be a hint of care. After half an hour he felt he must go back to his pitch, as his income depended on his sales.

As the days went by, F and Steve met more frequently, Steve paying for the drinks on one occasion, and she having mixed feelings of almost maternal care for him. She was curious about Steve's situation. As their friendship developed, she thought it best if they went to eat and drink together at different locations to reduce the risk of gossip. She had never been a gossip, and certainly did not want to be the subject of it. The small town where she lived had its share of busybodies, and the last thing she wanted was for this information to get back to Dyke or the children.

At their sixth meeting – or was it the seventh, she had lost count – Steve appeared with a somewhat crestfallen face! 'I'm being thrown out of my lodgings,' he blurted out. 'I'll be back on the streets again next week.'

'Oh, no,' responded Felicity.

'Yes, that smart chap I met at the station the day we met happens to be the brother of my landlady, and he put the boot in.' Steve was almost tearful as he faced a very uncertain future. Felicity drew in a deep breath.

'You could…' she paused for an overlong moment. 'You could…' she repeated, 'come and stay with me and the children. On a platonic basis only,' she said firmly, and nevertheless hoping that other customers in the café could not hear.

So it was arranged. She had the use of the car for the day and collected Steve and his belongings, which did not amount to much, but were all he possessed in the world. Felicity had prepared the ground carefully with the children, explaining that Steve was just a friend who would be living in the spare room for a while. 'Until he gets himself sorted out,' were her concluding words.

Sophie responded, 'In the room DADDY was sleeping in?'

'Yes, the very same,' her mother replied.

'Does Daddy know?' was Sophie's next question.

Back in Lyme Regis, the holiday was a disaster. First of all it rained much of the time, and on the Wednesday morning when the sun did shine, they all – except Steve who was still in bed – went off to the beach, but after an hour a big cloud came over and they had to find shelter from the coming thunderstorm.

Mrs Palmer was kindness itself. She had run the guest house

for more than 30 years and had seen every kind of human being come and go. Felicity had explained the situation, and Mrs Palmer had found a box room for Steve. He was grateful for a comfortable bed and accommodation, albeit a little small. The holiday had been largely paid for by Felicity's mother who, of course, had no idea that Steve would be going with the family. However, Felicity's contribution paid for Steve, although it was a move about which she was beginning to have doubts, not least because he never got up for breakfast – something which not only aroused the children's curiosity but that of the other guests as well. He did rouse himself at about 11am and went outside for a fag, but he never asked himself where Felicity and the children might be.

The receptionist at the small museum was very helpful. She was always delighted when children filled with curiosity arrived. She explained that tumuli were often called barrows. 'We have a barrow in our garden,' piped Freddie. 'It's full of weeds! Mum's always saying she must empty it, but she never does!'

Mrs Perkins was very patient and explained that this was a different kind of barrow, which seemed to satisfy Freddie. She went on to explain that older ones are long and straight and the more recent ones are round.

'What does "recent" mean?' It was Sophie's turn to be inquisitive. 'And what is the Bronze Age about?'

'Well, Sophie, it was about 2,500 years ago when people first made tools of metal instead of stone.'

'Wow! Even older than Grandma!' was Sophie's response.

Mrs Perkins was now in full flight. 'Look, here's a map. Can you see Lyme Regis? Here we are, and here is a long hill at Fort Walditch and tumuli at Lamberts Castle, and here at Chideock.' Mrs Perkins was delighted. She didn't have many visitors to her little empire, and certainly not with such enquiring minds.

One afternoon they got in the car to go and see some of these strange landmarks. Steve, however, said he would wander down to the promenade and may be back at supper time. With no father to play football with Freddie or to keep Sophie amused, it was proving, for much of the time, to be a rather humdrum vacation for Felicity.

In desperation, on the Thursday afternoon, which was damp and drizzly, F implored Steve to look after Sophie and Freddie for an hour so that she could have some 'me' time. He reluctantly agreed, and found them in the lounge busy with puzzles and drawing books, with one or two of the residents looking on with no small delight. Once again Steve felt superfluous, but as he had agreed to stay, he felt he must oblige, even if the other people in the room thought it an odd arrangement, since he did not look old enough to be the children's father, and he had a somewhat detached attitude to his charges.

Smartening herself up, F decided that a little window shopping would be in order just for an hour. A week's holiday with two children who were, for the most part, bored, plus Steve, made her ask herself, why did I ever bring him, and answer almost immediately, I couldn't leave him at home, could I? What if Dyke had come round and found him there?

She wandered up the main street of Lyme Regis, admiring its variety of shops and quite old buildings, when she spied a small notice in a greengrocer's window. It said, 'Is Your Life in a Mess?' The notice was really just leaflet size and said that at the Landslip Church, Archdeacon Sadie Selworthy would be speaking about her prize-winning leaflet called *Is Your Life in a Mess?*

What on earth was an archdeacon? She noted that the meeting was the next evening but hesitated to ask anyone where Landslip Church might be. She asked herself, Is my life in a mess? Here am I, a single mum trying not very well to bring up two children, deserted by my husband, and now involved with this guy Steve! Here we are in a lovely town but I've nothing to do but gaze into shop windows in the rain. My life probably is in a mess, but I for one am not going to admit it!

For a brief moment the rain relented and she found a place to sit, first making sure it was tolerably dry. She fished in her pocket and found a cigarette which she had pinched from Steve when he wasn't looking. She hadn't smoked for some while, but this roll-up would do. She lit it and looked out to sea. Somehow the taste of the cigarette seemed different and she could not inhale deeply.

'Lovely view,' said a little man with what she guessed was a Dorset accent as he joined her on the seat outside the little café.

'Yes,' replied Felicity in a non-committal way, and then, after a long pause, 'Those cannons – do they actually fire?'

'They did once. Lyme was a port with a harbour nearly as important as London; that's why it needed defending.'

Another couple of puffs on the cigarette and Felicity was feeling somewhat light-headed and woozy. 'You alright, love?' asked the stranger.

'Yes, I will be in a moment. Do you know what I want to do?'

'I've no idea,' said her companion.

'I'd like to take that gun and blow my husband's bloody head off.'

The man seemed only slightly perturbed. 'And the other gun?' he asked.

'I'd use that on Steve!'

'Who is Steve?' asked her companion, still appearing to be unshocked by her statements. Then he added, 'And what if there were a third gun?'

'I'd use that on myself!'

'Wouldn't that be a bit drastic?' replied the man.

Felicity was quite high by now, but she was just about able

to explain who Steve was. Then she said, 'I'd better get back to the boarding house; Steve is looking after the children.'

'Your children?!' said the man with a degree of incredulity. 'You've left your children in the care of someone you don't much care for?'

'I had to get out on my own for a while.'

'Tell you what. I'll get us a cup of tea and then take you back to where you're staying.' In no time at all he was back with two cups of tea. By now Felicity's head was beginning to clear and she realised the cigarette she had taken must be cannabis! After another 20 minutes or so she felt well enough to take up the offer of a lift.

She got out of the car at the guest house. 'Thank you very much. I don't even know your name. Mine is Felicity – but I prefer to be called F.'

The stranger shook her hand and said, 'I'm just a local friend,' and with that he drove off.

F need not have worried about the children as they were busily engaged in all sorts of puzzles. The other residents had made sure they were in good care, especially old Mrs Butterworth who had been coming there for the past 40 years and had continued to do so since her husband had died. She and her husband had always chosen the half-term holiday since they had no children of their own and delighted in those of other people.

The children looked up and barely acknowledged their mother, as they were so engrossed in what they were doing. Steve was nowhere to be seen.

The dinner gong rang and they all went to wash their hands. F made sure she changed her clothes to get rid of the smell of the 'cigarette'.

'Did you have a good afternoon, Mummy?' It was Freddie's turn to be curious.

'Yes, very interesting, thanks,' was F's flat reply.

Steve joined them halfway through the meal, but as usual he ate very little and almost played with the food around his plate. This was something the children did not approve of, since their mother had taught them that while other people in Africa starve, they should be grateful for their food and eat it all.

'Someone stole my fags,' Steve commented rather vaguely to no one in particular. F thanked him for looking after the children. 'No problem,' he replied, which she knew was a lie since he had left them and gone off goodness knows where.

Friday was the last day of their holiday. They managed to spend a short time on the beach later in the day when the tide went out, and the harbour and the fishing boats were of considerable interest. Steve, as ever, got up late, skipped breakfast and went off on his own.

As they were going back to the guest house, F spied another little notice in a shop window: 'Is Your Life in a Mess?' She felt as if she were almost being pursued by it. So, later, she discreetly asked Mrs Butterworth two things: first, would she check that the children were OK – their day had been tiring and they did not need any encouragement to have an early night – and second, where Landslip Church was.

'No trouble, dear. I'll pop in around 8.30 to make sure all is well. As for Landslip Church, just go up Exeter Road and turn left. It's quite a climb but it's easy to find.'

It was indeed easy to find, although it did not look like a church but more like a run-down hall. F checked the time and waited around the corner until exactly 7.30pm, and then she slipped quietly through the door.

There were about 20 people present, mainly elderly, although there were one or two teenagers. She sidled into the back row, trying to look as invisible as possible and hoping no one would greet her. Then, to her surprise, a little man walked to the front and introduced himself. It was the stranger who had befriended her the day before! 'I'm Pastor Nugent and I would like to welcome you all here tonight.'

'We know who he is,' muttered one of the teenagers, who had in the past week made the pastor's daughter the object of his attentions, without much luck.

The pastor continued, 'It's my pleasure to introduce Sadie Selworthy who, as you know, once ministered in this lovely town. Before we listen to her let us sing – how about the one we learnt last Sunday – "Praise Him, Praise Him, in every circumstance, Praise Him in melody and dance"?'

F wished the ground would swallow her up, and even more so when a lad of about 18 stepped forward and tried to belt out the tune. It was clear that he hardly knew it, and that his guitar-playing days were in the future rather than the present.

After the torturous singing, with which only about half of those present joined in, and certainly not Felicity who was trying to hide in the back row, Pastor Nugent caught her eye and smiled – something to which she felt she could not respond.

Sadie began by saying a little about herself and how she had come across hundreds of people whose lives were, to say the least, rather messy. She spoke clearly and with authority. F listened attentively, but with one eye on the door in case she felt the need for a quick exit. Sadie stressed that whatever the situation there was real hope, now in the present, and in the future.

'Not b... well, for the likes of me, or Steve for that matter,' she muttered under her breath.

Sadie spoke for ten minutes or so, and then Pastor Nugent said, 'Let's sing another song and then, after a cup of tea, Sadie will answer any questions.' This was the trigger F was waiting for: as quickly as she could, she dashed out of the door and rushed back to the guest house. A quick enquiry of Mrs

Butterworth confirmed that the children were OK and sound asleep.

Soon she went to bed herself, although she slept fitfully, and her last thoughts before she dropped off were, 'What does that Sadie know about us?'

The journey home was uneventful. Freddie pointed out the tumuli and Sophie, in her most authoritative voice remarked, 'You know, they are Bronze Age, more than 2,500 years old.'

Steve said almost nothing until they were nearing the railway station close to home. 'Can you stop here, please. It was a lovely holiday, thank you very much. I must be on my way.' With that he nipped out of the car, went round to the boot, grabbed his tatty old rucksack, and before any of the others could draw breath he had disappeared across the concourse. A furious honking behind reminded F that she had stopped in the taxi rank and had better drive off quickly.

Another surprise awaited them on their arrival at home. Dyke was standing on the drive with a bunch of flowers in his hand. 'Daddy!' The children could not contain their excitement. There were lots of hugs and tears.

'I've been a fool!' said Dyke.

'So have I,' replied F.

He said, 'There's a meal ready for us all. Your mum and I have prepared it.'

If F was overwhelmed before this, she was doubly so now.

'You can sleep in the spare room,' said Sophie with great authority.

'I don't think I want the spare room, thank you young lady,' replied Dyke.

Much, much later, F whispered in Dyke's ear, 'Well, why did you come home?'

'Well, quite by chance, I met your friend Zoe who told me

about the Skids Club at the local church. I suddenly realised how much I miss you and the children. She asked me, "Do you know that old hymn, 'God is working His purpose out'?" I said I had no idea, but she replied – and you know how earnest she can be – "I think God might be saying something to you."'

As Felicity wrapped her arms around him, she murmured sleepily, 'God is…' but before she could form the sentence she was asleep, dreaming, 'God is.'

The measure of a man

Sebastian, as was his wont, spent time reflecting on his life, his upbringing, his happy childhood spent with three siblings, their comfortable middle-class home in South Harrow. He observed his parents' happy marriage, his charming wife Louise, his son Nigel, who was now studying economics at Cambridge, and so on, but at the back of it all, a persistent nagging doubt persisted: Am I the man I should be?

His mind went back to the changing rooms at school, where teenage boys would compare their anatomies, and he was often teased because his male organs were much smaller than his contemporaries. However, throughout their married life, Louise had never commented, much less complained. Indeed, their physical relationship was all that a married couple should enjoy, and yet...

He had laughed at sitcoms on the telly where Frank in *Some Mothers Do 'Ave 'Em* often used to say to his wife, 'I'm a man, Betty,' when clearly he portrayed a less-than-macho image. He recalled a radio programme from his childhood called *The Glums*, where Eff often taunted Ron for his lack of masculinity, often made worse by the bombastic outbursts of Eff's father Glum Senior.

Louise was always wanting him to stand up to their bullying neighbours across the street, and to try to get a better job where he, instead of others, could be in charge. However, the last thing Sebastian wanted was to be 'in charge'. Domestically, over the years, Louise had adopted this role. It was she who organised finances, booked holidays, employed workmen when they were needed, and did more than her share of bringing up Nigel.

Sebastian thought up all sorts of excuses. Usually it was, if that's what Louise wants, then I'm happy. His job in computing kept him away from home quite frequently. It paid well, and much of the time he did not need to have contact with other people. Yes, if pressed, he was content, but still the doubts existed. Louise was always trying to cast him in the 'hero' mould – her 'knight in shining armour', except the armour did not always fit and was rarely shining.

As Sebastian ruminated on his life he wondered if religion had anything to do with it. His parents were Roman Catholics with strong views on abortion, contraception, etc, but they rarely went to Mass. Sebastian had come to reject these attitudes, even more so when he met Louise, who described herself as a 'Christian Agnostic'. In this sense they were little different from many of their neighbours: Christians in the vaguest terms. As Louise's father used to utter frequently, 'I'll always help my fellow man when I'm asked; doesn't that make me a Christian? It's the way you live your life that counts.' Sebastian, who had heard this many, many times, wanted to say something about faith and belief in God, but quietly demurred to his father-in-law, despite Louise's looks which said, stand up to him!

So life proceeded on its way, with Sebastian wondering if he might be in for a mid-life crisis, whatever that might mean. His inner turmoil, largely hidden from family and friends, was indeed a crisis that he found difficult to resolve. He had recently been to the library and borrowed a book called *The Female Man*, where the author, a self-styled American guru, encouraged her male readers to get in touch with the feminine side of their nature. Dr Josephine Haggety-Bowen ('call me Dr Jo') had flaunted her qualifications (which eventually turned out to be bogus) and made considerable sums of money through her publications and seminars that she called 'Becoming a Real Man!' Critics said her techniques were crude and rarely produced the results her clients expected or required. Nevertheless, she attracted large numbers of men who paid to see some of their number both humiliated and over-praised. Her skills were indeed seductive, and many a male was convinced of her genuine desire to help.

'Hi Dad!' It was Nigel on the phone. 'Thought I'd come home for the weekend, is that OK? Sunday's Father's Day so perhaps we can do something special.'

'OK, yes, fine,' was Sebastian's rather limp reply, completely forgetting that they had agreed to see Louise's father that day. Who comes first? This was always a dilemma in their household – Nigel or the overpowering father-in-law. It was eventually agreed that they would see Louise's dad after a pub lunch, as they wanted to spend as much time as possible with Nigel.

Nigel duly arrived and was bursting to tell his parents his news about life at uni and about his friends, especially Liz, whom he had met the previous term. Sebastian and Louise were dying to know all about Liz. Where did she come from? What was she studying? How old was she? Did he have a photo? What about her family? And so on. After an hour or so of gentle inquisition Nigel said, 'I've something else to tell you. My room-mate is called Gordon, and he comes from Glasgow. We play rugby together, though he's a better player than I'll ever be. He also drags me along to church.'

'To church?!' both his parents uttered in amazement.

Nigel continued, 'I'd like us all to go to church on Sunday, as it's Father's Day.'

For Sebastian this came as a shock. He always enjoyed receiving gifts on that day, even though more than once he had thought that commercialism perverted the occasion. Maybe going to church could restore some integrity to it all.

Sunday morning arrived and both Sebastian and Louise were more than a little nervous at the prospect of going to church. Sebastian considered whether he should wear a suit, but eventually settled on a blazer, flannels and a tie. Louise was in even more of a dither about clothes and changed her mind several times before Nigel shouted up the stairs, 'Mum, Dad, are you ready? We'll be late!'

Sebastian came downstairs and couldn't believe what he saw. His son was wearing sandals, shorts and a QPR football shirt. He couldn't envisage such attire to go to a place of worship. He was just about to object when he remembered that Nigel was now grown up and, from his modest income, had bought his father a suitable present to celebrate the day.

They duly arrived at All Saints, a few seconds before the service started, and were greeted by the welcome team. Sebastian noticed that many of those in the church were young and dressed very informally. He said to himself, I didn't know females with bare midriffs and crop tops were the order of the day in the Church of England!

His thoughts were interrupted by a nudge in the ribs from Louise, who intuitively guessed that he was more interested in some of the young women than in singing the first hymn.

What do I do with my hands? he thought. No hymn books or even a Bible to hold – it's all on the PowerPoint screen. How different it used to be when I was young. He solved his problem by holding on to Louise with one hand and keeping the other in his trouser pocket. He endeavoured to adopt an air of casualness, even if inside he was knotted up with nerves.

When the time came for the sermon, it was witty, informed and took as its theme 'The Measure of a Man!' Here we go, thought Sebastian, back to comparisons in changing rooms and the sports club. Such thoughts soon disappeared, though, as his attention was gripped by the speaker asserting that real men are not created by prestige, sporting prowess, bully-boy tactics or by their everyday abilities, but by their standing before God. He was particularly struck by the thought that small men (such as himself) could be big in God's eyes.

The service over, they opted out of church coffee – in Sebastian's eyes it would mean engaging in conversation with strangers whom he hoped he might not see again – and they hurried off to the pub. Nigel had been very quiet in church and had been watching his parents out of the corner of his eye. Embarrassment had given way to semi-involvement, and at the close he had heard his father say, 'Well, that was different!'

They enjoyed the pub meal, which Louise insisted on paying for. Then, with a feeling of dread, they all made their way to her father's house. 'Happy Father's Day,' smiled Louise when eventually the door was opened, and she deposited a present on his table. 'Thought you would enjoy this.'

Louise's father made a pretence of not wanting a present, but was soon tearing the wrapping paper. It was his favourite whisky, which at times was his only comfort.

'So what have you been up to, young Nigel? Is all that university knowledge coming out of your ears? What, what?' Nigel knew his grandfather well enough to reply that it had been a good eight months and that he was catching the train back to Cambridge as soon as they left.

'We had a nice lunch at the Crown after we had been to All Saints,' responded Nigel.

'Didn't invite me,' was the brusque response.

'To the lunch or to church?' Louise enquired.

'Both,' was the haughty reply, 'though I don't care for the latter. Bet you had a good roast meal; all I had was some of yesterday's leftovers.'

Louise's guilt was there for all to see. It was Nigel who saved the day. 'Sorry, Granddad, not to have included you, but you know it has sometimes been embarrassing – I stress, sometimes – when you've come with us in the past. Being rude to the staff doesn't help customer relations, you know.'

For once, Louise's father was lost for words. Sebastian wanted to say something, but in deference to and admiration for his son he kept silent. How was it that Nigel, at little more than 20 years old, was so adept at assessing a situation and saying the right thing? Louise's words about standing up to her father continued to haunt him as they said their goodbyes and hurried to take Nigel to the station.

As the train came in, Nigel kissed his mother goodbye, gave his father a big hug (which he had never done before) and with his mother's words, 'Bring Liz next time you come home,' ringing in his ears he settled down to travel back to his studies.

Early the next morning, the phone rang. It was Louise's father. Now one thing that never, or very rarely, happened was her father using the phone.

'I... I...' he was unusually hesitant. 'I... I... just wanted to say what a nice, charming young man Nigel has become, so different from his rebellious teenage years. What made him change?' Before Louise could draw breath to reply he continued. 'Was it this religious stuff that made him change? After all, he nearly became a dropout. How many times did he get into debt? How often did you and Seb bail him out? What about the time you had to haul him out of that squat? It's a wonder he ever got to university.'

'Look, Dad,' Lou interjected, but her words were lost and she got no further as her father was now in full flight.

'I can tell you I changed my will a year ago. Not a penny was going to him to be spent on drugs and booze.'

Again Louise tried to say that Nigel had never been on drugs, but yes, the drinking had got out of hand a couple of times. 'OK, Dad,' she sighed. 'I must go; I need to be at work in half an hour.'

However, her father was not quite finished. 'I just want to

add,' his tone now much more moderate, 'just because I changed my will, it doesn't mean I can't change it back again. Have a good day!' and with that the call ended.

Louise sat down in a state of mild shock. Her father really trying to communicate with her was wonderful. He had always said that every thought, every action, every word had financial implications. He should know, after 30-plus years in the banking world. Certainly it seemed that Nigel's earlier behaviour, and now his change of heart, had financial strings attached. What, she wondered, was in her father's will? That he had a substantial sum she had no doubt, but what did it contain? Would there be much for me? Her thoughts were interrupted by the clock chiming and reminding her she must be on her way to the playgroup where she was deputy leader.

'Had a good day?' asked Sebastian at the supper table. The question had, over the years, been asked more out of habit than any real interest, which had disappeared long ago.

'Yes, I certainly did.' Sebastian's ears pricked up and he looked at her with some curiosity. 'Dad rang up before I left this morning.'

'Your father?' His voice came out at a higher pitch than he intended. 'Your father?' he repeated in a more moderate tone, before adding with a note of sarcasm, 'What on earth did he want? We only saw him yesterday.' And after a pause, 'He never phones. Didn't he like his Father's Day present?'

Louise, who was busy dishing out the food, replied, 'He seems to have been struck by the change in Nigel since he went to university. He's probably going to change his will back again, having cut Nigel out some time ago. I don't know what's in the will. He said all along he has left the bulk of everything to me; after all, I am his only child.'

They continued with their meal, but the conversation soon ground to a halt. After supper, Sebastian muttered something about going to his study and catching up on the day's emails. Louise piled the plates in the dishwasher and switched on the TV. She barely glanced at the news; what happened in the world was of little interest to her, but something caught her attention and she sat bolt upright and screamed for Sebastian, 'Hey, Seb, come and look at this!'

He rushed downstairs, such was her cry, anxious to know the source of her agitation. The newsreader was explaining that Mr Brindly Jacobson had been taken into police custody, accused of provoking a riot outside the town hall! A sense of panic and dread overcame her. 'We must go and see him at once. I'll get the car.'

All thoughts of a quiet evening were gone as they sped towards the local police station. A very pleasant PC met them at the door and directed them to the duty sergeant who, without looking up, said simply, 'Next' (it was nearing the end of his shift and it had been a long, tiring, day).

'We're here to enquire about Brindly Jacobson,' said Louise hesitatingly.

'Why?' he had still not looked up from his computer.

'He's my father.'

'Oh is he?' came the toneless response. 'Identification?' Still the head did not look up.

'I'm afraid I have none, at least none to show that he's my father. What is he being charged with? We only saw it on the local news and it wasn't clear what it was all about. The TV didn't show who it was, only gave the name.'

At last Sergeant Davies looked up. 'When he came in he was charged with being drunk and disorderly, but the superintendent says we'll be adding violent conduct to the charge sheet. These offences are not little ones, you know.'

They reeled in shock. Brindly, a 72-year-old pensioner, charged with such activities – it was totally out of character. Summoning up strength which she did not really possess,

Louise asked, 'Are you sure it was Brindly Jacobson?'

The sergeant hunted in his desk and produced a bus pass, which had obviously seen better times. It was old and faded and the face on it was obviously male, but it was very difficult to make out any details other than it was bald and what was left of the hair was grey. It could be almost any man of a certain age.

'Did he have any other ID on him – something with his address?' Louise was becoming bolder.

'Nope, just a bus pass,' was the non-committal reply. 'We'll check with the local council in the morning as to the last address of the holder. He was too drunk to give us an address.'

'Can we see him please?'

'OK, you can look through the opening into his cell. He's probably still sleeping it off. We'll give him a couple of hours before we question him again. Atkins!' He called the PC who had been at the door to show them down to cell 3. 'Don't wake him,' he warned. 'You know how violent he was when we brought him in.'

'Yes, Sarge.' The trio made their way down to cell 3. PC Atkins let them look into the cell and there, lying on his side, was a bald-headed man with straggly side locks. The smell of stale alcohol soon reached Louise and she thought she was going to vomit.

'That's not my Dad!' she shouted. The man in cell 3 did not move. PC Atkins closed the opening and they hurried back to the sergeant at the desk.

'That's not my father!' Louise was puzzled and distressed.

'Isn't it?' the sergeant was still his laconic self. 'We've fingerprinted him, but he's not on the database, so who is he?'

Sebastian, who had hardly said a word during the whole proceedings, said, 'Look, I know it's getting late, but why don't we ring Mr Jacobson to see if he's at home. If he is, that'll solve all our problems.'

Won't solve mine, thought the sergeant, thinking that his professional conduct might be called into question if he were to put his thoughts into words. 'You can use our phone if you like.'

'No thanks, I'll use my mobile. I'll try outside.' As they made their way out of the station they elicited a weak smile from PC Atkins as they went.

Brr. Brr. Brr. The telephone in Brindly's home rang and rang. He had retired to bed at 9.30pm with his pills and a glass of whisky, which meant he was able to sleep through anything. Also, the telephone was in the kitchen downstairs so it was far enough away for almost anyone not to hear it.

Louise was beside herself. 'Dad's not there,' she exclaimed. 'Where is he? He's not in custody and he's not at home. Where on earth is he?'

It was Seb's turn to take the lead. 'We'll have to go round to his house. If he's there he'll be angry, but at least we'll know where he is. If he's not there we'll come back to the police station, right?' Seb had an annoying habit of saying 'right' when he tried to exert his masculine authority, such as it was. They got in the car and made their way to Brindly's house.

Seb hammered on the front door while Louise went round the back, but all to no avail. They made enough noise to disturb some of the neighbours, in what was quite a close-knit community. Lights were going on in some bedrooms and a voice called out, 'What's going on? We want to get some sleep!' One or two people began to join them, and before long a small crowd had gathered. Wilf appeared dressed in his boxer shorts; it was a warm night. Tracy, the single mum from two doors down, appeared in a translucent nightdress which made Wilf's attention and eyes turn from the conversation.

'I'll get a ladder and you can climb and knock on the bedroom window,' said Wilf, turning his attention back again to the situation at hand.

Seb banged on the front door again but there was still no reply. Louise was frantic – if the man in the police station was not her father, and her father was not in the house, where was he?

A couple of minutes later, Wilf staggered across the road with a ladder. 'Will you climb or shall I?' he enquired, secretly hoping Tracy might be willing. Seb agreed to climb the ladder. Now Wilf was not known to be a man of finesse and decorum, as one or two dents in neighbours' cars and a big scratch on his gatepost bore witness. Nevertheless, he tried to position the ladder conveniently against the wall, only to smash the bedroom window.

'Say, can you do that again for the camera?' boomed a voice out of the darkness as a TV van arrived, equipped with spotlights. The small crowd had now grown and would doubtless continue to grow if people thought they might be on the telly.

Sebastian, drawing himself up to his full 5'4", felt it was time to take charge of the situation. Louise felt proud of him. 'Ladies and gentlemen, we are very sorry to have disturbed you, but we are very anxious about Brindly. We know he's not too popular around here, but we went to the police station as we understood someone claiming to be him had been arrested. However, it was not him, and this is why we are here.'

'Couldn't you have waited till morning?!' a voice shouted in the dark.

Sebastian ignored him and said, 'Perhaps everyone would like to go home. I'll climb up the ladder. The TV lights will help me see inside the bedroom.' A couple of reporters were sent to interview neighbours, the younger male making a beeline for Tracy; and in the glare of the spotlights Sebastian started to climb the ladder.

Just at that moment a small, bald head appeared through the broken glass window, blinking in the glare of the lights. 'What the hell is going on?' shouted Brindly, rubbing the sleep out of his eyes. Some of the crowd, who had grown somewhat disinterested, cheered while others simply grunted, but all were amazed by the sudden appearance at the window.

'What a great shot,' shouted the TV director. 'Let's get down to the police station and get their side of the story.'

'Couldn't you have used the keys you keep?' shouted Brindly, now fully awake. Suddenly Louise remembered that the keys were in her handbag, and she ran to the car to retrieve them. Sebastian gingerly climbed down the ladder, thanked Wilf for his help, and went in through the front door with Louise. Within minutes the cul-de-sac had returned to its former nocturnal peace. However, the lights stayed on in Brindly's house for quite a while as explanations and apologies took place.

Refusing the invitation to go back with Louise and Sebastian to their home, Brindly retired to the back bedroom, thinking about the insurance claim he would have to make the next day. Secretly he felt quite proud of his son-in-law.

It was 2am by the time Sebastian and Louise arrived home. As they got into bed, Louise wondered, is this the measure of a man, or is there something more? She remembered something the preacher had said about being big in God's eyes.

Lou whispered, 'Who do you think was that man in the police cell?'

Came the sleepy reply, 'Don't know. Perhaps we'll never know. Been an interesting time since Father's Day!'

'Very interesting,' was the reply.

The damp BBQ

Ben and Jan loved barbecues. Every spring, as soon as it was warm enough, out it came. Ben, of course, regretted that at the end of last summer he had forgotten to clean it out – damp had got into the charcoal remains and the grill not only had last year's grease on it, but also six months' growth of mould. He waited till Jan was out of the house, scurried to the garage and managed to get it all cleaned up before she returned home.

'Here you are, darling – sausages and burgers,' she said. 'What have you been doing?'

'Oh, nothing much,' was his vague reply, already thinking ahead to the evening when he could be crowned 'King of the Grill'.

Their summer holiday had been long planned and Ben, ever the map expert, plotted the route to a campsite in Luxembourg. 'Never been to Luxembourg,' he declared with authority, not bothering to enquire whether his wife had other ideas. 'Look, this site at La Rochelle has an all-weather pool,' he continued, 'and it looks great in the brochure.'

Ben was a good father to his children, who were now away at university, but he was the sort of person you could never argue with – at least, not in public. Jan never thought of herself as long-suffering or downtrodden, but she rarely contradicted Ben's ideas, which flowed thick and fast.

So they found themselves on their way to Luxembourg, with 'Have a good holiday Mum and Dad' ringing in their ears, and Jan expressing a desire that nothing calamitous would happen while their protégés had the house to themselves. After various stops en route they arrived at the forested site and soon had their motorhome in place, electricity connected, awning extended, and table and chairs in position underneath it.

The weather was for the most part cloudy, so they settled on sightseeing in Luxembourg itself and its various castles. However, on the Thursday there was a definite improvement in the weather, so they spent most of the time in the pool, which now had its sliding roof open to welcome the sunshine. By the evening it was still warm and pleasant so Ben announced (he was good at announcing) that it was BBQ time, and out came the stand and the portable BBQ, which was duly lit while they enjoyed an aperitif.

'Harrumph,' a guttural voice interrupted their relaxation. 'Smoke, smoke,' the voice grew louder and had a certain edge to it.

Ben thought, yes, BBQs do smoke a bit when they're first lit. So he moved it and hoped that would be acceptable. Apparently it was not, so he moved it again. However, their neighbour, although he was some distance from them, was not to be placated. He reappeared, this time waving his arms furiously, stopped only to pick up a large green watering can, advanced on to their pitch and proceeded to empty the watering can on to the BBQ!

Jan and Ben were both gobsmacked and stood there wondering what to do, as the retreating figure went back to his caravan.

'I'll pull out his electric cable. I'll let down his tyres. I'll...' began Ben.

Jan bravely looked him straight in the eye. 'Do nothing!' was all she said. Ben, his masculinity dented on two sides, reluctantly agreed and nodded his head. He reflected later that this was not the first or even the second time he had experienced a damp BBQ. There was the time at the annual Round Table summer gathering when, in the mist and drizzle, he had stayed outside and cooked burgers and sausages on his much larger kettle BBQ. Someone did eventually saunter out with half a pint of lager to offer a 'Well done, old chap!' He had not cared to enquire whether the remark applied to him or to the meat which was cooking more slowly than he had expected, not least because every time he opened the lid, drips from his hat fell onto the contents.

The second occasion was at the Scouts' parents' do. Everything had begun well, but a sudden thunderstorm had left him stranded. Even Jan had left him to it. Some remarked how noble he was; others thought him a fool, but did not express it. Shouts of 'Isn't it ready yet?' and 'We're starving in here!' didn't help, but nobody actually came and poured water on his cuisine.

Later that night, Ben was still feeling rather sore. Jan told him she had seen their neighbour emptying waste at the drinking water trough, and thought he might be a troublemaker.

'You might have warned me,' replied her bruised spouse.

As they went to bed Jan remarked, 'Doesn't it say somewhere about loving your neighbour as yourself?'

The sleepy, unenthusiastic reply was, 'I'm sure there's an exception for camping and caravan sites!'

'Did you both have a good time away?' Tracey opened the door as they returned after a long and weary journey, having negotiated the jams on the M25 and M4.

'Yes, super, darling,' was Jan's response, wide-eyed at how clean the house was, with lots of beautifully arranged flowers.

'Didn't meet any nasty men, did you? I had a dream about a big guy trying to knock Dad down.'

'Strange, but as a matter of fact, we did,' replied her mum.

After the story had been told, it was Tracey's turn to be shocked. 'Gosh, Mum, are you alright? Did Dad fight him off?'

'I would have thumped him good and proper,' intervened

Ollie, who had been listening to the conversation. 'What good would that have done? Luxembourg is a peaceful country; as far as I know they've never been at war with Britain, and we didn't want to be the people to start one,' responded Jan with more than a hint of sarcasm, trying to close the conversation and get round to preparing supper.

'Mum, don't bother with supper. Ollie and I are taking you out. You must be tired after that long journey. It's our thank you for putting up with us during our hols.'

'It was lovely having you around again,' responded Ben, adding with a wink, 'not that you were here most of the time.'

At the Red Lion they surveyed the menu and made their choices. 'Not opting for the beef in BBQ sauce then, Dad?'

'No, not tonight!'

Later that evening Ben and Jan expressed their gratitude to their children who had, in their eyes, grown up. Ben ventured the observation, in an almost philosophical tone, that family meals like the one they had all just enjoyed were becoming rare occurrences. 'I don't know when the four of us will sit round a table again.' The remark was greeted in silence, but not the silence of distress, just the feeling that this type of family meal might not occur again, at least not until Christmas, if even then. Ben and Jan were very aware that many of their friends would normally just eat TV suppers, which they thought seemed to inhibit conversation and lead to stunted family life.

'Wasn't it really, really, nice of our two to take us out for a meal?' said Jan as she got into bed, but the only reply she received was a loud snore.

The next day Ben took their two offspring to the station, Tracey to get the train to Birmingham to resume her studies in media and politics and Ollie to Dundee to finish his last year in geology. Jan's parting words were, 'Goodbye, Ollie. Go and see the medics if that headache gets worse.'

'It's nothing, Mum; I think I probably had too much to drink last night.' Jan didn't think it was that, but she had noticed that some paracetamol had disappeared from the medicine cupboard.

At church the next day both Ben and Jan noticed the sudden drop in the number of young people in the congregation, but it was generally accepted as part of the ebb and flow of church life, at least in their church.

Back home, Jan had rung Ollie on his mobile but there had been no reply. 'That's funny,' she reported to Ben.

'What's funny, love?' he asked, barely looking up from the sports pages of his Sunday paper.

'I've tried ringing Oliver again, and there's still no reply.' She hoped that using his proper name might evoke a greater response from her husband.

'Probably in the student bar with his friends.'

This seemed to satisfy Jan as they sat down to Sunday lunch, on their own for the first time since the beginning of the holidays.

It was gone midnight when their phone rang. 'Who could that be?' asked a sleepy Ben.

'Answer it and you'll find out,' came his spouse's reply.

Ben had complained long and loud about nuisance calls, but still, in spite of Jan's insistence, he had done nothing about it. Nevertheless, he picked up the receiver and grunted, 'Yes?'

'It's Ninewells Hospital in Dundee. Dr Laird speaking. Is that Mr Ben Prentice?'

Oh my God, thought Ben, Ollie's been involved in an accident.

The calm Scot's voice at the other end of the phone sounded very reassuring. 'I am very sorry to tell you that your son Oliver is in intensive care. We are doing various tests. He collapsed at the student bar and was brought in three-quarters of an hour ago.' By this time Jan was at Ben's side trying to catch what was being said. 'We think he has a brain tumour, but as he had been in the bar we have to wait a while for the effects of the alcohol to wear off.'

Ben was now wide awake, 'We'd like to come and see him.'

'Of course,' replied the reassuring voice, 'but it won't be easy at this time of night.'

'We'll make some arrangements.' After discussing Ollie's condition and prospects of recovery, which did not sound too hopeful, the conversation ended.

Ben and Jan wandered downstairs in shock and made a cup of tea, trying to take in the situation. Jan, looking desperately for something to focus her mind and emotions, suggested looking on the net and, after much searching, they found a flight from Birmingham to Edinburgh, and from there a train to Dundee.

'Let's pray about it,' Jan said as they started to pack and prepare for their trip.

'What good will that do?' said a shocked Ben, who was going through one of his brief but regular agnostic phases.

'It'll help to calm our nerves; we can't do much else now.' So she prayed as only a mother could, wondering in her heart of hearts what the outcome would be.

The journey to Birmingham in the early hours was uneventful – few people were on the road – as was the flight to Edinburgh. On arrival they rang Tracey to let her know what was going on, and also rang Mrs Armstrong next door to say they had needed to go away urgently.

'Business, I expect,' was Mrs A's response.

It was a very weary couple who arrived at the hospital. They had barely spoken throughout the journey; their minds were full of all sorts of thoughts. They had managed to doze a little, but fear of what they might find at the hospital dominated their feelings. The staff nurse took them to the room where Ollie was lying, and they were shocked at the sight which greeted them. Before long she ushered them into an attractively painted side room. 'Dr Laird will be with you in just a minute.'

They sat down, holding each other's hands. Ben couldn't help noticing a Bible on the table in the corner. Dare I go and open it? he wondered. His thoughts were interrupted by Dr Laird entering the room. His face told the whole story, and he told them, 'Oliver is deeply unconscious. I very much doubt if he has long to live. I say this with great hesitation, but we will need to consider whether it is right to switch off his life-support system.'

'Oh no,' gasped Ben. Jan was just as shocked and did not really respond.

'Now,' said Dr Laird, 'why don't you go and get something to eat, sleep on it and come back later. I'll call in Dr McFarlane and we can meet tomorrow. If there's any change I'll ring you.'

Neither of them felt like eating, but merely nibbled at bits in the hotel restaurant. The waitress hovered attentively and was puzzled by their behaviour.

Jan rang the church pastor who promised to ask other church members to pray about the situation. Ben wondered what good that would do, even though he secretly admired his wife's constant faith, whereas his was so up and down and so much related to circumstances. In his heart of hearts he wanted a Christian life that was firm and constant, but it just would not happen.

They retired to bed, but sleep would not come as they thought of Ollie hovering between life and death.

Morning dawned, grey and damp. Then, before they were really awake, tensions which had been simmering below the surface revealed themselves. Jan said very calmly, 'I think we should let him go to be with the Lord.'

'Let him go! How can you, as a mother, say that?!' said a horrified Ben, thinking of all the times he had gone fishing with

Ollie, how they had gone to watch their favourite team QPR, how he had taught him to swim, and so many other happy memories. 'No! No! No!' he shouted, loud enough for the guests in the hotel bedrooms nearby to hear.

A knock on the door made them pause in their altercations. Ben answered it. A young woman stood there, 'Is there anything wrong?' she asked politely.

'No, no, not really,' answered Ben hesitatingly, holding the door ajar just enough to see the woman's face. This seemed to satisfy her.

He closed the door and turned to look at Jan, who very wisely said, 'Let's go down to breakfast and behave ourselves.'

'OK,' grumbled Ben as he headed for the shower. Breakfast was almost as silent as the dinner had been the evening before. The same waitress wondered what was wrong and expressed her concern to the manager, who duly came to their table.

'Good morning,' he said brightly. 'Is everything alright?'

'Yes, yes,' replied Ben curtly, then he realised he was being a little rude. 'The food and the service are excellent; it's just that we have to make some key decisions today.'

'Alright, Sir, I'll leave you to enjoy your meal,' the manager replied, thinking that's their business or, more likely, they are getting divorced!

They soon returned to their room where Jan insisted on reading from the Gideon Bible that was in the drawer, and praying for Ollie. Habakkuk 3:17-19 was Jan's favourite passage in times of crisis and she read it out loud to Ben who was only half listening – if that.

They returned to Ninewells Hospital. Ollie's condition appeared to be unchanged. Then at 10am, in a comfortable side room, they met with Dr Laird, who introduced his colleague Dr McFarlane. Staff Nurse Currie was also present, but she stayed in the background. Dr Laird explained the situation in detail, trying to keep the medical terms as simple as possible, and then went through the options. Dr McFarlane put it very bluntly: Ollie had no real hope of a meaningful life and would be in a permanent vegetative state for the remainder of his days. Withdrawing life support would be both realistic and for the best.

'You really mean like putting a dog down. We had to do that to our beloved Bernie!' Ben was almost shouting.

'Calm down, darling,' whispered Jan. 'We haven't come to that yet.'

But Ben, his emotions at fever pitch, was not to be denied. 'My guess is that you want Ollie's bed; he's taking up space in your wretched hospital!'

Dr McFarlane, whose steely grey hair matched an even more steely posture, interrupted him. 'It's not quite like that.'

'What is it like, then? He's my only son, and I love him. I love him.' Ben collapsed in tears.

His discomfort was interrupted by a knock on the door. 'What is it now?' Dr McFarlane was in his most brusque mood; he had many patients to see and he wanted to sort out this situation as soon as possible.

The door opened and the Sister returned, saying hurriedly but gently, 'I think you should all come quickly.'

Arriving at Ollie's bedside, Jan quietly murmured, 'I think the decision has been taken from us,' as they viewed Ollie's lifeless body.

'The Lord gave and the Lord has taken away,' breathed Dr Laird. 'I'll inform the chaplain if I may.'

'Yes, please do,' replied Ben and Jan in unison. Dr McFarlane had now left to be with his other patients.

After a while, when Tony Anderson, the on-call chaplain, had met and prayed with them, they returned to the room that was set aside for relatives to discuss and agree certain formalities. The staff nurse was the model of kindness and understanding. They returned to sit for a while with Ollie, who was now free of all the gadgetry that had kept him going during these last hours.

'At peace,' was all Jan could say, and eventually they left and made their way back to the hotel.

Ten days later, the funeral back at St Agatha's was moving and dignified, and not without moments of humour and joy. Many of Ollie's friends came, even though some of them felt a little uncomfortable at the expressions of Christian hope that were highlighted in the service by all taking part.

Twenty years later

Ben had retired from his job as sales director and Jan had gone back to teaching part-time, which she enjoyed. They were grandparents: Tracey had married Richard, and they had two lovely boys. Ben's retirement pension was more than adequate and they were able to enjoy many things, such as extended holidays, which had not been possible in the past. However, they avoided both Luxembourg and Scotland because of the painful memories which were associated with these places. Ben joined U3A and an art appreciation class. They considered moving to a smaller house, but always at the back of their minds was, 'This was Ollie's home.'

Jan was as committed as ever to the church family and worship, but Ben had stopped going soon after Ollie's funeral. 'Where was God when I needed Him?' he would say in the early days after Ollie had died. The minister and other members of the church came to visit and enjoy meals together, but all to no avail. The minister moved on and his replacement arrived. He was very different – much more academic, but had a kindly heart. He, too, prayed with Ben and had lengthy debates with him, but got nowhere. Jan was constant in her love for Ben, but she was lonely.

At one U3A meeting Ben met Eve, who was a widow in her mid-fifties. She was quite attractive, and Ben was drawn to her. His imagination ran riot. Eve was everything Jan was not – flirtatious, but not in a provocative way. They talked over tea and after the meeting it seemed only natural to continue the conversation in Eve's car. Ben told her his life story in about 30 minutes, especially about Ollie.

All the other cars had gone and they were left alone in the gathering dusk. A knock on the car window indicated that the caretaker wanted to lock up. 'You want to be 'ere all night? We've 'ad people like you 'ere before; disgusting I call it,' he said. Ben and Eve were shocked, and Ben quickly got out of the car and into his own.

'May I have your number?' he asked.

'Here's my card,' smiled Eve as she started the car and drove off. Ben stared at the card and read 'Eve J Rue, Women's Fashion Editor, *Warwickshire Herald*, 70779 511106 email Evefish@pinmail.co.uk'.

Ben could not believe it. Was Eve genuine in her concern for him or was she just another journalist out for a quick story? He'd had enough of those when Ollie died.

He drove out of the car park and stopped in the nearest lay-by where he studied the card more carefully. She was attractive and younger than most of the other U3A members. He put the card where he thought Jan would not find it, and drove home.

Jan, immersed as always in community and church activities, greeted him at the door. 'Have a good meeting darling?'

'Yes, it was OK.'

Since Ollie's death he had found personal communication increasingly difficult. One-to-one talking, even with Jan, he found painful, but with Eve it had been different. With her, conversation just flowed and flowed. He felt very easy in her company. He hesitated a day or two before dialling Eve's number. She answered immediately, but not without a hint of breathlessness in her voice. She was obviously very, very busy, but she still had time to listen to him.

'Could we meet again? I'd like to take you out to dinner. I can't wait until the next meeting of U3A,' he said.

'I was delighted to meet you, Ben. You're an engaging man, but I'm not a U3A member. If you look at your programme you'll see I'm the speaker for next month. I just came along to see what happens and check out PowerPoint and the other facilities. You'll see from your programme that the subject is "Taking the lid off the world of fashion".' Ben was lost for words.

Eve seemed to be everything that Jan was not, but he eventually said, 'OK, I understand. I wasn't planning to go to the next meeting anyway. It's been good meeting you; you're very kind. God bless. Goodbye.' He fished in his pocket to find the U3A programme and realised that Eve Rue was indeed scheduled for the next meeting. He then searched around the car and, to his horror, could not find her card!

It troubled him for a few days, but then he settled back into his retirement routine, which he found was regulated but lacking in the engagement which work had involved. However, he could not get Eve out of his mind, but now he had lost her card. Where had it gone, he wondered? He had no means of contacting her. He knew where she worked, but he discounted that approach.

One day Jan said quietly, 'I think I'm going to give up work completely so that we can have more time together.'

'That would be wonderful, darling.' He still called her darling even though, in some ways, their relationship was a good deal cooler than it used to be. Jan felt that the causes were more complex than the fact that they were getting older.

His next comment was less enthusiastic. 'I suppose it's so you can spend more time at that church of yours.' He had long ago given up any thought of it being 'my' church, and his annual visit at Christmas was more out of sufferance than joy.

Jan felt she had to be at her most diplomatic. 'Well,' she hesitated, 'as a matter of fact...' She paused.

'Go on,' he said, trying to be patient, but feeling irritation welling up inside him.

'You know that room at the side of the church building?'

'Yes,' Ben was trying to be both interested and calm, but felt that he was not doing terribly well at either.

'The vicar has been in touch with the local council and they're willing to support the idea of a centre for the homeless, and he's invited me to help run it!'

'Good God,' Ben exclaimed, without realising what he had said, and then, after a pause, added, 'If that's what you want to do, good luck I say, but don't give me any more of that "we can spend more time together" rubbish.' With that, he left the room abruptly.

After a day or so he had calmed down, half apologised, and even took a mild interest in the project, which got off to a somewhat shaky start. A reporter from the local paper got wind of it and the following week the banner headline read, 'St Ag's to be a doss house for down-and-outs'. As a result the church secretary was forced to write a letter explaining what the plans were and that a full consultation exercise would be carried out.

The following week, the paper printed a corrective statement, albeit on the inside page. However, there was a variety of contributions to the letters column, both positive and negative. The latter included a letter from Lt Col Nicholas Pendelton-Hough, saying, 'What on earth is the Church of England coming to?'

However, the majority of decision-making bodies were in favour. Money was donated and raised. Jan approached local businesses for support, and within six months a room with four single beds, a small kitchen, a bathroom and toilet, as well as a little lounge/TV area had been created. Members of the church worked their socks off' to get it all ready in time for the grand opening, with the chairman of the council and the bishop in attendance. The reporter from the local paper came, and the following week a very different report appeared: 'Bish tries out bed in doss house!' it read, but apart from that it was quite positive.

All it needed now were some residents. One of the other problems was the need for someone to sleep in and provide breakfast. Sam and Craven from the church offered to do two nights each. 'But what about the other three nights of the week, let alone holidays?' This was Jan's voice at the church council.

'Can you do it?' was the response, so Jan raised the matter with Ben.

'You can't doss down on the floor like Sam and Craven. I won't allow it!' he responded.

'Why can't we use our motor caravan? I could park it immediately next door. Problem sorted.'

'It seems so,' was Ben's weary response.

So that was the arrangement until a part-time administrator with sleepover duties could be appointed. Adverts were duly sent out. Then the first residents arrived. A man in his late sixties was brought in by his social worker, and then another. As the people arrived, so did the money. Residents were not required to pay for their board and lodging, but an appeal and a 'giving Sunday' brought in quite large sums. Although the request did not go out to the wider public, money did come in – including, surprisingly, a cheque for £100 from Lt Col Pendelton-Hough, who had been at a dinner with the chairman of the council.

The third resident was a young man of 20 who had been homeless since his stepfather had kicked him out. He settled in well, found a part-time job as a cleaner and made great efforts to help in the hostel.

In the course of conversation with Ben, Jan ventured to say that she would like to introduce the young man to him.

'What, bring him home here?!' he exclaimed.

'Only for a meal.'

'Oh, all right then. What's the layabout's name?'

'Oliver,' Jan replied. There was a shocked silence.

'Oliver,' responded Ben. 'I can't believe it – the same name and age as our dear Ollie when he died!'

So Oliver came. He was the model of politeness, though he was puzzled when Jan said grace before they ate. He had never seen that before!

Oliver said very little. It was years since he had sat down at a table for a meal. He looked around him; there were pictures of Ben and Jan's wedding, of Tracey and the grandchildren, and some, a little faded, of a young man about his own age. He was very curious but held his tongue.

After the meal they played Scrabble, which was something else that was new to him, but which he enjoyed. Later, Ben drove him back to the hostel.

'Thank you, Sir.'

Ben was taken aback to be called 'Sir', but brushed it aside as Oliver got out of the car.

'Darling,' Ben knew what was coming. 'I've been thinking. Could Oliver come and live here with us? We have a spare room.'

Ben thought for a moment, especially about being called 'Sir' more than once. As an attempt to make a very weak joke he said with Dickensian gravity, 'Please, Sir, can I have some more? Ha! Ha! Ha!'

'This is too serious a matter for jokes, even as feeble as yours.'

'Can we pray about it?' Now it was Jan's turn to be shocked:

It was 20 years since they had done that!

So Oliver moved in. He had little by way of worldly possessions. The manager at the hostel was pleased as there was now a waiting list for places. On the first day, it being a beautiful evening, Ben surprised Jan by suggesting a BBQ – something they had not done for many, many years. In fact, they had done little together since Ollie had died. When they brought it out, it was rusty and covered in cobwebs, but still usable. They enjoyed eating al fresco. Oliver had never enjoyed such hospitality, let alone such a fine BBQ.

'Shall I pour water on it and douse it?' asked Oliver as they finished their meal.

'No, don't!' shouted Ben, loud enough for the neighbours to hear. 'It's alright, I'll explain another time. Let it die out on its own.'

As they were settling down for the night, Ben said suddenly, 'I love you, Jan, and I admire you. I would like to go to church this Sunday, and take Oliver with us.'

'What a wonderful idea,' she replied. 'By the way, I found this card in the motor caravan. Who is Eve?'